FEVER DREAMS
OF A
PARASITE

Advance Praise

"*Fever Dreams of a Parasite* is a collection filled with stories of inequality, toxic masculinity, economic disparities, the weird, the cosmic, the gritty, the visceral, the beautiful and the uncomfortable. Every word and sentence act as fingernails scraping under the skin, with every story an unsettling that rattles and shakes, filled with monsters both literal and those wearing the skins of humans. Iniguez brings us into worlds where there is a cannibalism of the human race both literal and metaphorical, where mirrors of our own world exist along with the shadows that lurk which we refuse to acknowledge, and show us how the world often skins us alive and leaves us to dry, to shrivel, before it wears us on its bodies called society, called nation, called humanity."
—Ai Jiang, Bram Stoker Award-winning author of *Linghun*

"Savage, brutal, harrowing and riveting. Pedro Iniguez has created a nightmare collection of stories filled with unexpected twists, disturbing plots, unforgettable characters and ghastly settings. Each story is a sleep murderer. This is true horror; horribly gripping."
—Nuzo Onoh, "Queen of African Horror" & Bram Stoker Lifetime Achievement Award Recipient

"Porn stars, hitmen, hunters, and the innocent wander deserts both frozen and aflame. Literal talking heads and cosmic intestines abound. Rites and rituals ancient

and modern ensnare even as they liberate. Iniguez's *Fever Dreams of a Parasite* will infect your soul with no cure in sight. Here are wonders and woes that will be with you for a long, long time. Enjoy."
—Theodore C. Van Alst, Jr. Bram Stoker nominated editor of best-seller *Never Whistle at Night*

"Among a rising tide of excellent contemporary horror, *Fever Dreams of a Parasite* seized my attention. Watch out for Iniguez."
—Laird Barron author of *Not a Speck of Light*

"Pedro Iniguez's gifts to you are monstrous people and things that might replace you, haunt you, eat you, or just toy with whatever you thought you were. You might even be the last sacrifice Iniguez has planned in this shiver-inducing collection."
—Nicholas Belardes, author of *The Deading* and *Ten Sleep*

Published by Raw Dog Screaming Press
Bowie, MD
First Edition

Cover art © 2024 by Daniele Serra
www.DanieleSerra.com/
Book Design by Stephanie Pearre

Printed in the United States of America

ISBN: 9781947879850 / 9781947879867
Library of Congress Control Number:
2024951817

RawDogScreaming.com

FEVER DREAMS OF A PARASITE

stories by
Pedro Iniguez

RAW DOG
SCREAMING
PRESS

Also by Pedro Iniguez

Control Theory

Synthetic Dawns & Crimson Dusks

Mexicans on the Moon: Speculative Poetry from a Possible Future

Table of Contents

For Taylor Grant
Your kindness will live on. We shall meet once this fever dream is over.

Introduction

by Cynthia Pelayo

A parasite is a living organism that worms its way in, digging deep and taking up residence inside of a different species, and there it takes up space, in a place it does not belong. Parasites wreak havoc. A parasite feeds off of the host they've burrowed into. They generate a distortion, causing sickness and chaos. Parasites like the trouble they orchestrate, delightfully so. In *Fever Dreams of a Parasite* by Pedro Iniguez, parasites are things – the uncanny and supernatural, and people as well who set into motion a series of events that disrupt and remain with us long after the story has concluded.

Very often the worst kind of parasite is a person. People as monsters, monsters as monsters, things that cannot quite be explained are also monsters, and in this collection Iniguez explores them all.

The power here is in the moments, in the distortion. That is what Iniguez presents in these creeping terrors that linger once they've concluded. There's almost this film we can feel between our fingers, this sticky substance, this layer of dust with us that remains long after the story has ended. In *Fever Dreams of a Parasite*, the uncanny is deeply and effectively on display. Think *The Twilight Zone*, *Tales From the Darkside*, and even a hint of *The Outer Limits*, where the world becomes tilted on its axis and then reality dissolves around you. In these stories, everything begins as normal, a woman driving along the road at night on the way to a party, a clothing designer contemplating his next creation, a mother and daughter needing to make a phone call in the night, until reality becomes distorted. It's the switch from normal to the surreal that happens so quickly in these stories that leaves one breathless.

11

When these moments happen, this is when horror is more pronounced, when the thing that is lurking in the night reaches out to grasp us and we cannot even contemplate what it is or explain its existence, because there is just no time, because the monster is here, and it is upon us. When someone is worried for their life as a monster looms over them, the last thing they care to know are the origins of that monster. They just want to live, and this is horror, and many of these characters do not survive. Horror author and educator Tim Waggoner has said the most effective horrors do not overexplain. The monster just is. The threat is just there. And Iniguez delightfully celebrates that rule here in this collection.

The nods to cosmic horror, H.P. Lovecraft, Thomas Ligotti and John Langan are ever present. Yet, what's most striking are juxtapositions between race and class and the influences of Lovecraft. Like Silvia Moreno-Garcia, or Victor LaValle, Iniguez has taken concepts of cosmic horror as popularized by HP Lovecraft—who was famously hateful and racist—and incorporated commentaries on the lived experiences of diverse people, namely Latino and Mexican Americans. This makes Iniguez a part of this wave of diverse authors exploring a cultural reckoning of Lovecraft's work.

Lately it seems as though Iniguez has been writing like he's running out of time. Iniguez is a Rhysling Award finalist and a Pushcart nominee. His fiction and poetry has appeared in *Nightmare Magazine*, and various anthologies and he recently released a collection of poetry titled *Mexicans on the Moon*. His works have foundations in horror, but confidently expand into other realms, namely science fiction fantasy, and of course poetry.

There's quiet in his work, and a playfulness, perhaps fanciful even. Yet, when the horrific is presented on the page, it's as if the reader can feel a cold grip reach into their chest. In this collection, we see difficult situations become much worse, like in "Nightmare of a Million Faces." "Feast of the Dreamer" is philosophical and fantastical, yet wholly ghastly.

"What must someone do in order to reach a place of peace and joy."

In "Skins" we see that "There was nothing out here but pain and emptiness…" "Shantytown: A Mexican Ghost Story" is quiet, but powerful nonetheless, and there is so much more. We see machinations of manipulation, when one is used as a tool to have an opinion swayed, the fantastical—where brother and sister are prey, sea creatures and folk stories, heartache, the lost and the broken, and more. Iniguez also plays with time periods, and of course, humans as the monster.

This is a wide-ranging collection, but the terror that keeps the reader slowly turning the pages is the possibility of a threat, which we all experience in life, the reality that something can become catastrophic within minutes. The threats here come swiftly to both baffle and horrify.

The mind of Iniguez seems vast and eager to explore worlds and realities, monsters that are grounded in folklore, the cosmic realms above, or that stare us back in the mirror. Either way, the stories here will certainly delight and offer the explorations of a confident author setting forth on a journey to create so much more.

—Cynthia Pelayo, Bram Stoker Award-winning author of *Vanishing Daughters*

Nightmare of a Million Faces

When the sun plunged beneath the horizon, the striations of red clouds looked like gashes raked across the sky; flayed wounds ready to rain blood on a thirsty desert. Anastasia Mendez glanced at her left forearm. The lacerations crisscrossing her skin had mended but the scars would always be there; mementos etched upon flesh.

She brought her attention back to the steering wheel and swiveled her head trying to find the road she'd veered off some time ago. She squinted her eyes as if that might help, but the creeping darkness had obscured much of the world around her. "Damn," she said through gnashing teeth. At some point, she must have nodded off and lost her bearings as she was prone to do on long drives.

Joey Garrett, infamous porn producer and self-described King of Smut, would be mingling at a Halloween-themed wrap party tonight. A party she needed to find if she had any hopes of getting a job and paying off her crippling medical debts. They had accrued over the last few weeks, a tumultuous time marked by medical procedures that had left her hollowed out and sutured like a jigsaw puzzle. The dislocated shoulder, the gashes, the broken nose, the split lip, the abortion…

She clenched her teeth and fought the urge to sob again. *No. Snap out of it. You need to find this party*. But the search had proved fruitless. In that darkness, everything looked the same. A world enclosed by jagged hills and loose boulders, the flatland stretching between, densely forested with scrub and yucca. A far cry from the glimmering lights of Los Angeles, there was something otherworldly about the desert that made the hairs on the back of her neck turn prickly.

Her nails dug into the steering wheel as she eyed the dashboard clock: 7:00 P.M. She hoped there was still time. *Relax*, she told herself. *The night's young.*

She plucked her phone out of her clutch and checked for directions. *GPS Signal Lost.* The connection had probably severed sometime after that rest stop in Joshua Tree.

What the hell would she do now? She'd never driven down this way before. The roar of cars had long subsided behind those obsidian hills, and there had been no landmarks, no lights, no strips of blacktop to lead her to safety. She was all alone out here.

Instinctively, she eyed the rearview mirror. Her taillights projected red wisps into an ocean of black. Her heart thudded against her chest and her breaths became shallow gasps. She didn't know what she expected to see. Perhaps, Robert tailing her in his Corvette. No. He was likely already at the party, waiting for her. For a moment she felt silly; she thought she may have been overreacting. But deep down she knew she wasn't. He wasn't beyond that. He wasn't beyond anything. She'd found out the painful way.

As night fell, she tried to shrug off her anxiety, but the Prius' headlights did little to mitigate the encroaching darkness. Before long, the windshield had fogged over as her panic-filled breaths warmed the car.

She pulled over alongside a boulder at the base of a hill and popped the brakes. "Just breathe," she said, closing her eyes. She inhaled deep breaths through her nose, and exhaled with her mouth until the pounding in her chest subsided. Just like her therapist had coached her.

"Okay," Anastasia said, scooching out of the car, "let's figure this out." A breeze swept across the desert, caressing her face with icy fingers. A chill spread across her arms and legs. Tonight, she'd worn a plain white V-neck, black leggings, and open-toed wedges. A decision she was swiftly regretting.

Maybe she could get enough of a signal to call Monica. She raised her phone in the air. "Come on," she said through chattering teeth, "give me something to work with." Nothing. She considered turning back; there was a chance she could catch a major road back to L.A. if she headed back the way she came.

No. She was tired of running. Of giving up. She'd be strong for once and stick it out. Besides, she needed this in the worst way. Admittedly, an Airbnb in the middle of the Mojave Desert wasn't her idea of a great time. But Monica had pressed her about coming to the party, an effort to get her out of the house after all that had happened.

After considerable prodding, Anastasia had relented. She told herself it'd be a way to get in touch with a few producers, schmooze her way back into a few films. After that it wouldn't be long before the money started to come in and she could reclaim her life, start all over again. Make up for the horrible things. The things she'd lost.

Resting a hand on her belly, she told herself her decision wasn't selfish, just honest. There came the familiar tingle in her nose again as a thin film of moisture coated her eyes. She never even knew if it was a boy or a girl. What could she do? She was an unemployed porn star left to fend for herself in a world waiting to devour people like her. She couldn't do it alone; certainly not with Robert facing time in prison. A lump formed in her throat. She had loved him. She had wanted to leave the industry, start a family. But he had other plans for her.

Anastasia was nineteen when she met Robert Pierce on her first shoot, some low budget casting couch video. She'd been a nervous, trembling wreck when the cameras rolled, her skin a canvas of goosebumps as Robert's hands explored her body. In between takes he had comforted her, promised to guide her along, show her the ropes. Before long they'd started dating, eventually moving into a condo together. He offered to be her manager, to steer her clear of predators and sketchy contracts. Young, soft spoken, and alone in a new city. How could she refuse?

She could still hear his voice. "We're going straight to the top, baby. Stardom, money, drugs, book deals; anything your pretty little face desires."

She thought he loved her, but coveted was more apt a term. She knew now. She was just a prize to be won, a marionette to be controlled, a means to an end.

He'd been in Florida shooting some films while she decided to take some time off. At first, she hadn't thought much of the subtle changes happening to her body; the modest weight gain, the swollen feet. But the trip to the doctor's had proved an unexpected revelation. The news had been a pleasant shock. A welcome development in their relationship, one she thought had been blossoming over the years. She saved the surprise for his return, watching his face intently for an elated reaction, but it had only seethed with rage.

Her fingers slid across the raised scars on her arm.

The memories flooded back, intrusive little things bearing gifts of pain and shame. She recalled everything, like a movie reel playing in her mind. The belt came down on her, slicing her arm open like raw meat as she tried to block his onslaught. The weeping wounds stung as if hot coals had been pressed to her skin. Then his fists shattered her nose and parted her lips like the Red Sea.

17

Her neck suddenly began to flare like it did the moment his fingers had laced around her throat, depriving her of air. Her jaw clenched and she wrapped her arms around her chest. The thoughts had once again manifested into phantom pains.

With the tip of her middle finger, she wiped the tears from her eyes. Leaning against the hood of the car, she regarded the sprawl of Joshua trees laid out before her, their twisted forms like devilish entities watching her in the dark. Judging her. Waiting to admonish her. She considered the possibility that Robert might be hiding there amongst the scrub, watching her too.

She clutched the door handle.

She paused when she spotted what appeared to be old petroglyphs etched onto the boulder beside the car. Curiously, she approached the rockface, squinting as she tried to decipher the images chipped onto its smooth surface. In the dusk, the sepia-colored markings were almost indiscernible.

There were rudimentary depictions of bighorn sheep, coyotes, and bobcats lurking amidst the scrub and grass. A dome of spiraling stars speckled the top of the image, beneath them swaths of yucca trees, where in their shadows lurked an uncanny form; a great thing with numerous heads protruding from a long, snaking body. Some of its faces depicted animals or people; others were too terrifying to fathom.

The pictures were mesmerizing, the gravity of their mystery pulling her toward the rock. Were they religious depictions? A story of some sort? Somehow, she had the gut feeling that she'd stumbled on a secret most eyes were not privy to. Hesitantly, she traced her index finger along the contours of the many-faced aberration.

The phone suddenly vibrated in her palm, snapping her out of her trance. *GPS Signal Restored.* A wave of relief washed over her as a broken green line directed her toward her destination. *Thank God.* She wasn't far.

Anastasia slid back into the Prius and drove, reuniting with a narrow dirt road leading south. After a few miles, the path terminated beside a small house overlooking hundreds of vacant acres in every direction. Through the car's frosted windows, the house looked solemn, like a specter keeping watch over the desert, its eyes and mouth aglow in fire.

Several Cadillacs and BMWs had been stationed on either side of the house. She parked on the fringes of the property, just outside the amber glow of a pair of floodlights. She threw on her leather jacket and stepped out. The place was a small single-story home, its patio flecked with lawn chairs, benches, and a fire pit. The clapboards appeared a freshly painted beige with no signs of sunbaked erosion.

The subtle scent of woodsmoke lingered in the cool air. As she approached the house, she could see that the hill had been scorched. Gnarled and crooked, the remnants of yucca trees stood as obsidian obelisks in the dark, their bark singed bare. Fresh saplings had started to sprout from the dead land, their blades swaying in the wind like sea anemones. Something crunched under her feet. She lifted a heel. Ash and small bone fragments carpeted the ground like gravel.

She dusted the ash from her heels on the planks of the patio and entered the house. Greeting her was an ankle-high haze of dry ice, the cloud hovering lazily across the living room. A creaky wooden floor announced her arrival. Two dozen costumed partygoers awash in red light mingled in the living room, their chatter mixing with the beat of electronic music. A few masked guests cast sidelong glances her way before returning to their conversations.

A swell of blood rushed to her head as her eyes darted from person to person. She spotted some familiar faces. A few strange ones as well. She wiped the sweat from her palms against her thighs. Would he be here? Robert had been in many of the same films as the talent in the room. Hell, he'd fucked most of the girls here. Girls who'd worshipped at his feet like acolytes, a god of their own creation.

Howling laughter broke out toward the center of the room. Cassy Kane, dressed in a revealing pirate costume, twirled drunkenly as a crowd of men cheered her on. Amongst the spectators was Joey Garrett, garbed in a wolfman outfit. He regarded Anastasia and smiled, his lips curling crookedly. She would make her way toward him, introduce herself. But first, she'd find Monica, tell her she'd arrived.

Anastasia hung her jacket on a coat rack and waded inside. A man wrapped in rags shuffled toward her and plucked a bottle out of a Styrofoam cooler. "Beer?" he said in a muffled voice she could barely make out. She stepped back, regarded the contours of his bandaged face, and decided it hadn't been Robert. She politely waved the mummy off.

As she searched for Monica, she wriggled past Ben Dover and Jack Hammer, their arms flailing and feet shuffling clumsily to the beat of the music. There had been rumors Ben and Jack had been involved in sex trafficking, though nothing had ever been proven.

She averted her gaze. It wasn't the first time she'd been in a compromising position between both men, though not by choice. When it came to the industry, she had come to learn that she had little say, including who she'd fuck onscreen.

Ben and Jack were swathed in crimson silk vests and cheap Dracula capes, the smell of musk rotting the air around them. As she shimmied past, they eyed her blemished arm and offered each other fanged grins. Her face flushed with embarrassment. Everyone had known. She had made an earnest effort to keep a lid on things, but gossip metastasized like untreated cancer. This had been a bad idea. She should have stayed home.

Anastasia slipped past the crowd, hung a left, and strode into an empty kitchenette, slumping over the sink as her heart beat against her sternum. Dragging in long, deep breaths, she let the air fill her lungs and settle the fire coursing through her veins.

Get over yourself. You're a big girl and you need to talk to Joey. Maybe a drink of water would do her good. She plucked a small tumbler from a cabinet and turned the handle on the faucet. Nothing came out.

Long fingers suddenly wrapped around her left forearm. "There you are," said the voice at her back. Anastasia spun around to find Monica flashing that bright, bleached smile of hers. Wine glass in hand, she leaned playfully against the doorway dressed in a skimpy devil outfit, a pair of horns adorning her head. The corona of red light at her back enhanced the effect.

"God," Anastasia said, "you scared the fuck out of me."

"Sorry, Kid," Monica said, her fingers moving to her neck where her favorite pearl necklace should have been. "Forgot how jumpy you've been lately." Monica had taken to calling Anastasia *Kid* due to their ten-year age gap, though she was far from old. But at just thirty-four, producers had begun casting her in not-so-coveted MILF roles. The death knell in many a woman's porn career. At least financially.

Anastasia's eyebrows furrowed. "I'd say I've been more than just jumpy, Monica."

Monica's smile faded. "No. You're right, Kid. I'm sorry. I know it's been a rough few months. Listen, don't be scared. He's not here."

"Yeah," Anastasia said, her head stooping.

Monica removed her devil horn headband and strapped it over Anastasia's head. "Why aren't you in a costume, hunny?"

"Didn't feel much like dressing up," Anastasia said.

"Well, look," Monica said, brushing away a lock of black hair from her eyes. "We're gonna move the party outside soon."

"Monica," Anastasia said, "did you tell people about what happened?"

Monica wrapped an arm around her chest, bit her lip, and swirled her wineglass. "I may have inadvertently told a few people."

"What the fuck, Monica?" Anastasia said. "Nobody's gonna want to work with me. They'll say I'm that baby killer who ruined the great Robert Pierce's career."

"First of all, people in the industry get abortions all the time. Second, no one's surprised your boyfriend got locked up. We've all heard the stories. It's not just you he's dragged through the mud."

"He's not my fucking boyfriend," Anastasia said, the heat from her cheeks radiating outward. "And he's out on bail." Her fists clenched as she felt her legs tremble. Her breaths became quick and shallow. She felt powerless, unimportant. As always.

"I-I'm sorry." Monica set her glass down and stepped forward, her arms open for a hug.

Anastasia put up a hand. "No. Give me a minute. I think I need some fresh air."

Monica opened her mouth to speak but Anastasia slunk away through a screen door at the end of the kitchen. Outside, she shut her eyes and let her anger dissipate slowly into the cool desert air. There was no point being here. Nobody in that house gave a shit about her.

She opened her eyes. This side of the property overlooked the eastern portion of the desert, a vast nothingness staring back at her. Beneath the hill sat a valley, a deep depression shaped like a crater. It appeared out of place, not like something the Earth had gradually carved out over the ages through erosion or the shifting of tectonic plates.

A wisp of cigarette smoke wafted across her face, bleeding into the night sky where the moon cast a halo through a patch of clouds.

"Yeah," a voice said. "I have you booked for next week. Your family is gonna love this place." To her left, a man sitting on a small bench snapped his cell phone shut and tapped a cigarette, breaking loose a pillar of ash. He wore a reflective orange vest over a thick gray jacket. With a head of scraggly blonde hair attached to a long, oval face peppered with stubble, he didn't look like most actors she'd come across.

His mud-stained work boots grated back and forth against a patch of ashen dirt. "Prescribed burns," he said, meeting her gaze.

"I'm sorry?" Anastasia said.

"The desert's full of invasive plants. Not from around here, that is. They steal moisture away from the native grasses. It's a hot, dry world out here, so every drop counts." He tipped his head toward the scorched ground at his feet. "The county schedules prescribed burns to try to quell their spread."

"Oh," she said, instinctively crossing her arms around her chest. She checked the screen door. Monica was gone. "How do you know so much?"

"I work for the county." He put out his cigarette on the black soil and smiled warmly. He extended a hand. "Name's Riley."

21

"I see," she said, hesitantly offering her hand in return. "Well, nice to meet you, Riley. I'm Anastasia."

Riley shook her hand gently. "Not enjoying yourself inside?"

"Not really."

"Mind if I ask?"

She pursed her lips, thought about it for a moment, and supposed there'd be no harm in telling him. "Ex-boyfriend. Can't shake the feeling that he'll turn up any minute and…" She paused, unsure of how to finish the sentence.

Riley regarded her scars. "Hey, don't be scared. You're safe with me." He patted the seat beside him. "Here, sit down. I don't bite."

Anastasia forced a half-smile and nervously eased into the seat, leaving enough of a gap so their legs wouldn't touch. He stank of tobacco, beer, and kerosene. "I don't know why I'm telling you this, but I was pregnant. Four months in. He didn't take the news too well."

Riley shook his head in dismay. "I'm so sorry."

"It's not your fault. I'm used to men punishing me for living my life. God. And I let it happen. Guess I've always been a pushover." She peered at the sky, her eyes jumping from star to star. They gleamed like distant jewels and held the promise of better days. And yet, they were always out of reach. "Sometimes I wish I were stronger. That I could shed my old self and start over. A new life."

"Hey, don't say that," he said. "It's never too late to change things."

"Anyway," Anastasia said, "how'd you end up at this party?"

"I own the house. Run it as an Airbnb. I'm a friend of Joey Garrett, the producer that put this shindig together. I let him book the place for free."

"Why'd you buy a house in the middle of nowhere?"

"My grandfather built it in the '50s. My family used to live here until we moved into town just over yonder. There's only so much one can take living out here. It's a cruel place."

"I bet," she said gazing around the horizon, the moon illuminating the faint outlines of the peaks and canyons. A shooting star streaked across the sky and fizzled out somewhere over the crater. She made a wish. "Believe it or not, this is my first time in the desert. Been a city girl my whole life. My family never did much travelling."

"Count yourself lucky. You ever hear of the Pinto People?"

She shook her head.

"They lived in this desert about 8,000 years ago. Besides a few excavated tools,

22

there's not much known about them on account they just vanished one day. No one knows if they assimilated somewhere else or just died out here."

"That's wild," Anastasia said. The last part didn't surprise her. She'd felt so helpless out in the desert's dark expanse, like a stranger out of place. She couldn't fathom what it was like in the daytime at the mercy of an oppressive sun. "I could never make it out here."

"Whatever lives in this desert," Riley said, nodding, "has adapted to the cruelty of its harshness."

"I'll drink to that," Anastasia said. "Which reminds me, I don't have a drink. Listen, I have to introduce myself to a few people, but maybe we can keep this conversation going later? It's a hell of a lot more interesting than anything going on in there, I promise you."

A smile cut across Riley's face, his cheeks rosy in the dim light. "I'd like that."

Anastasia beamed as she got up and turned to open the screen door. She couldn't remember the last time she'd smiled and meant it. She'd spent so much time living in fear and grief that the memory of human contact had nearly faded like the petroglyphs.

Inside, she noticed the chatter had stopped, leaving only the sound of music blaring through the house. Red plastic cups and beer bottles littered the misty floor of the otherwise empty living room. She found the stereo and turned off the music. Silence.

"Monica?" Anastasia called out. No response. Maybe the party had already moved outside.

She went out the back door, where the hill faced south. Where there should have been chatter and music and rustling, there was only a subtle hum, the nocturnal whispers of the desert, and the faraway chirping of insects. The floodlights created a small crescent of illumination. Beyond its light stretched the expanse of night and nothing more.

No—not nothing. She could see a deeper darkness a few yards ahead. A ditch. She approached it cautiously, her feet dragging as she moved forward. She gasped and felt her heart skip a beat. Strewn alongside the rim of the ditch were heaps of wallets, undergarments, and assorted jewelry. Rings, sunglasses, a cheap cape, Monica's pearls.

First, her hands began to shake uncontrollably, then the shivers coursed down her legs. She forced herself to take another step. Within the ditch lay a tangled heap of shriveled limbs, dry and contorted as they interlaced with one another. Leathery faces peered upwards, their hollow orbital sockets staring back at her.

In the gloom, she couldn't be sure but there was something that seemed like Monica, its corpse like a discarded doll, its head a mop of black disheveled hair. Anastasia's eyes settled on the corpse's face. Those unmistakable bleached teeth had been bared in a lifeless grin.

Riley stepped outside holding a can of kerosene, a freshly lit cigarette dangling out the corner of his mouth. "Don't be scared."

Out in the darkness beyond the sphere of the house's floodlights, something rustled. Anastasia spun around. The thin shoots that had sprouted from the singed earth—not yucca, she was sure now—lashed out like feelers, prodding, grasping greedily at the air around her feet. She sidestepped their thrashing tips, tripped over her feet, and fell to the ground, breaking her fall with her palms.

Glints of moonlight caught on something jagged and rocky as it breached the earth, uprooting heaps of black sediment. The scant ambient light hinted at a colossal, appalling form as it flailed about in the darkness beyond. Its eyeless head sniffed the air with a bristling tentacled snout. Rows of sickle-like legs hoisted its long, segmented carapace as it lurched slowly forward. The nightmare could best be described as a cross between a centipede and a star-nosed mole; something not born of an arid wasteland. Something that had been forced to adapt to a new environment.

She wanted to run but fear paralyzed her legs. Her heart drummed against her chest and her lungs burned as they struggled to take in air. The monster let out a high-pitched screech and she felt a piercing pain in her head. Fragmented visions raced inside her mind as if something had been scanning her memories, forcing them to life. Memories of Robert. Of a child flushing out of her body.

That instant, Robert stepped out of the darkness holding a baby in the crook of his arm, its body tiny and dark and bathed in blood. "Hunny," he said. "Don't be scared."

Her unborn child cooed and cried. Her heart ached for her baby, and she found herself rushing toward Robert. She tried to pull the baby from his grasp. Only it wouldn't budge. As if it was attached to Robert's flesh.

Something was wrong. Up close, the child's face was blurred, smoothed over and devoid of features. It was nothing more than an abstract, a thought unrealized. She let out a pained wail. This wasn't her baby. She'd never even seen its face. She'd only gotten to know it from the pieces that had fallen out of her, sometimes one at a time.

Her chest heaved and she began to sob, the tears in her eyes distorting the world around her.

A pair of shoots sprang from the earth and coiled around her ankles, entrenching tiny thorns deep into her skin, locking her in place. Warm trickles of blood cascaded down her feet, pooling on the ground. Another pair of shoots latched onto her arms, gradually squeezing until they turned purple, and all sensation had been wrung from them. With a swift, cold sting, one tendril pierced her neck like a mosquito's proboscis. Anastasia gurgled as blood collected in her throat.

The monster screeched again, and the tendrils coiled around her body constricted. A swell of memories flooded up. Of the night Robert beat her. Of her father yanking out clumps of her hair. Of men having their way with her, discarding her, leaving their imprints, like bruises in her mind. She glared at the monster dwelling in the shadows. *Get out of my head*, she wanted to scream, but the tendril in her throat had robbed her of her speech.

The Robert-and-fetus hybrid shambled back toward the monster, a thin fleshy tether connecting them like an appendage. They were just facsimiles. Like the lure of an angler fish, they were bait.

A green sprout burst from the ground, its tip bloating and bulging into a fleshy pod the size of a melon. The pod swelled and something unraveled from within. Like rapidly expanding cells, clusters of meat began to form until something that resembled Anastasia curled naked on the desert floor, its body shimmering in fluid like a newborn baby.

Anastasia gasped and hacked as her naked duplicate began to drag itself across the dirt. The facsimile pushed off the ground with trembling arms. Then it stood with bowed, quaking legs, its balance supported by the tether coupled at her back. The facsimile was a perfect copy, even down to the scars marking her arm.

The sprout around Anastasia's neck tightened and her skin grew taut, her throat ran dry. The spittle on the corners of her mouth dissipated. A wave of nausea washed over her as her veins retracted and shriveled.

She heard Riley's voice echo in her mind. *It's a hot, dry world out here, so every drop counts.*

Her facsimile shuffled toward the creature in the dark. Once in the shadow of its corpulent shell, she turned to Anastasia. "Donbeescared," her duplicate said, its words raspy, garbled, a farce of a human pushing out air through a meat pipe for the first time.

"I don't think it's from around these parts," Riley said, his voice quivering with fear. He stood over the ditch, regarded the husks below, and doused them with kerosene. "But we've got a pact. The town keeps it fed, and it leaves us alone. I'm sorry. You know better than most. We've all got masters to appease." He flicked his cigarette into the grave and great flames spat skyward, lighting up the night.

The fire illuminated the veiled countenances of dozens of costumed facsimiles lurking in the shadows; puppets, lures, all of them tethered to the monster as it scuttled back underground.

In the shadows, the false Monica smiled at her warmly. As did Ben and Jack and Cassy and Joey and the rest of the partygoers. People she'd known. Others she hadn't. "Don't be scared," they said in unison.

"Don't be scared," Anastasia's duplicate echoed, her voice now a perfect match to her own.

Anastasia felt her eyeballs dry and wither, a thousand needles pressing into her pupils. The stars became great, blurry pinwheels before the world vanished from her sight. Arms and legs growing limp, she felt herself slipping, her death giving way to a rebirth, a twisted chance at that new life she'd always wanted. And yet she couldn't help but feel a deep ache in her heart knowing that the new Anastasia would be just as powerless; forever a pawn to yet another monster.

Feast of the Dreamer

Aurelio Treviño swatted the blowflies hovering ravenously over his face as he spotted the patch of loose earth. The ravine was nestled at the end of a beaten dirt road, hours from the nearest town. Amidst the dimming afternoon light, he looked around one last time to see if there had been any stray hikers lingering in the distance to bear witness to his transgressions.

Satisfied with his solitude, he speared the shovel into the mound of black soil and the ground beneath his mud-crusted shoes broke seamlessly. It wasn't long before the stench found him, the fetid scent of rot and sulfur burning his nostrils. He hawked a wad of phlegm, spit it out, and grimaced.

It will be worth it, he reminded himself. *The dreams will come.*

Staring back at him from the pit was the countenance of what might have once been a middle-aged woman, her patchy green-blue face sunken and gaunt, her brown eyes frozen into a thousand-meter stare. She was beautiful in her own way, despite the onset of decomposition. Many were. Beauty remained long after death, he'd found. He rattled off the thought and continued to sift through the earth until he caught sight of her naked torso, her bruised skin swollen, puffy like a balloon.

As he strapped on a pair of latex gloves, he thought about the woman, lifeless under his shadow. For years, the local cartel had used this plot of land as a dumping ground and there was no telling who she may have been: A sicario's trifling ex-girlfriend, a rival boss wife, a food vendor who refused to pay her dues.

On occasion, Aurelio used to make up stories about the people he buried, anonymous in their solitude. It gave them, in his mind, a semblance of a new life, imbuing them with a soul. It was the least he could do. Sometimes it helped repress the guilt. Most times, it didn't. This one, he decided, had been a vocal activist waging a righteous war against the narcos and the string of missing women in the state. A cause worthy of a crusader like her.

Before he'd given up that life, he'd had to put down many like her, nabbing them in narrow alleys, whisking them away in the dead of night, never to be seen again. He'd bring them here, of course, after a trip to one of the dozens of clandestine death houses seeding the state. He dwelled on all the torments he'd inflicted on them over the years as they squirmed and gasped and pleaded for pity, their shrieks powerless to change a thing.

He stooped his head and closed his eyes as he felt the familiar tug at his heart, the old feelings starting to consume him, gnawing away at him like an infestation of fleas on a mangy dog. And much like a dog, after some mild discomfort, he shook off the feeling and went about his business.

Aurelio unclipped a box cutter from his belt, knelt beside the woman, and sliced her open from sternum to navel. He counted himself lucky; he'd found her before decomposition had liquified her organs. Like fruit, the bodies couldn't be overly ripe.

He quickly flinched at the swell of putrid air and buried his face in the crook of his elbow, stifling a hacking cough. He wished it didn't have to be this way, lurking like a ghoul atop a shallow grave, watching as the maggots feasted on her organs. But this was the only way to traverse the chasm between worlds.

Soon, the dreams would come. Soon.

Reciting the Lord's Prayer never really helped much to cope with the ugliness of it all, but he did it anyway before he shoved a gloved hand into the cavity in her belly. He scooped out a moist lump of cold, viscous entrail—much like the innards of a carved pumpkin—and rattled off a fesw larvae, shoving his prize into his mouth.

Like fruit, he reminded himself. Nothing more.

Aurelio ended his feast alongside the flies and maggots just as the sun sank below the world.

There were eyes all around this dusty country, watching, waiting eagerly to report to their masters sitting on golden thrones in fortified palaces. When Aurelio was convinced he hadn't been trailed, he entered his room and fastened the latch behind him.

The roadside motel was small, tucked out of the way, and far from anywhere important. It would only be a matter of time before they found him and executed him for his delinquencies. He knew he couldn't outrun his pursuers forever, nor could he shut out the voices. Unless, of course, he fled where no one could follow—not even the ghosts of those he'd wronged. And there had been legions of ghosts, always skulking deep in the dark corners of his mind, murmuring amongst themselves, recounting his sins like bedtime stories.

Aurelio covered his ears with trembling hands until the voices faded into the ether.

The waiting was torment, the incubation period a drag through pain and sorrow-filled thoughts. In that time, he undressed, sat on the edge of his bed, and flipped through a bevy of scrambled television channels. Telenovelas, the local news, badly dubbed American films. Sometimes he would approach the window and peek through the blinds in bouts of boredom, the moon bathing the road in its pale blue light. A few times, he'd crack the door open and inhale the sweet summer air in anticipation of the ritual.

By midnight Aurelio felt the nausea form in the pit of his belly and quickly radiate up into his brain. As his head throbbed and his vision blurred, he flicked off the lights and rushed to light the candles on the nightstand. The sacrament brought him comfort. There was, after all, a sanctity to the process.

A fire flared throughout his face and his stomach churned in vile ways. Aurelio lunged into the bathroom, knelt at the gape of the toilet bowl, and expelled the contents of his toxic meal. The retch of gray chunks, bile, and blood stained the porcelain, pooling together to form a repugnant stew.

After he'd expelled the contents of his stomach for what seemed to be an agonizing stretch of time, he pushed himself up and peered in the mirror. Red eyes looked upon the raspberry blotches pocking his once-handsome face where the blood vessels had ruptured. He lay a hand on his head and felt the warmth of the fever running its course.

Every journey required self-sacrifice: The wrenching of his insides, the blemishing of his face, the scorching fevers. But it had always been worth the pain. Always. It brought him that much closer to the dream world.

Leaning against the bathroom doorway, arms wrapped around his chest, he broke into a sweat. Soon, the wonders would come to him once more.

Aurelio inhaled the stuffy air, shut his eyes, and saw the vague landscapes again, the eccentric orbits of dozens of moons dotting the night sky. He grasped out in front of him as if the sights were tangible. Though nebulous, the images from the dreamscape had burned themselves deep into his brain, ingrained into his eyeballs like the lingering ghost images from an old television set. But the visions were incomplete, fragmented, like peering through a shattered stained-glass window.

He needed to venture further. All the way.

What was clear though, was the voice echoing in his mind as it had in his dreams, beckoning Aurelio deeper into that darkness. A darkness tinged with pleasure. Yes. The Apostle of Bloat awaited. His voice had been deep like pools of black water, yet soothing like an aloe balm upon seared flesh.

The sound of tires rolling over gravel spurred Aurelio toward the window. "No, no, no," he muttered under his breath. A blue sedan wheeled slowly down the road until it merged with the darkness on the horizon. He could never be too sure if his pursuers had found him. When his heart settled, he sighed and sat on the edge of the bed, his eyes feeling heavier by the second. Almost.

Aurelio remembered vividly how he'd first stumbled upon that dreamscape after gorging himself on a meal of spoiled beef. The spell of violent vomiting had left him bedridden and at the mercy of fevered dreams. Dreams that allowed him to leave the pain behind forever. Dreams where he knew peace and pleasure and the stains of guilt had washed off his soul at last. But he knew better now. They weren't delusions but temporary traverses into another reality. A place beyond human understanding. The dreams were gateways.

After that mind-altering experience, Aurelio had sought to relive his voyage—craved it night and day like an addict. But to venture farther into that realm, he needed to sacrifice more of himself, to grow dire in illness, close to death. He spent months experimenting with rotten foods, and psychoactive drugs, his body exposed to varying stages of bacterial malady and self-induced fevers. During his explorations, he had discovered the secret lay in the ingestion of the deceased—the mortal fruit of the gods.

It began with roadkill, feasting on the burst intestines of small rodents on lonely stretches of highway. Then, it progressed to the rotten brain matter of mutilated cattle. All had wrecked his insides, his mind, carrying him further into that occulted realm. Tonight, he'd sampled the true fruit—the festering remains of a human corpse.

"Soon," Aurelio said, his voice coarse, his throat raw with flaring pain.

He crawled under the bedsheets, anticipating the sensory wonders, the splendors that awaited, where there existed a world of miracles and ecstasy and the sorrow that had eaten away at his insides like a brood of maggots would cease to exist.

Aurelio blinked and, from one moment to another, he had traversed into a different world. Sleep became a tether to another reality. Like a deep-sea diver plunging into unfathomable depths, he waded deep into an ethereal realm not meant for mortal beings. He stood, naked and cold, before a world of vast obsidian mesas and spiraling peaks. Chasms plunged into infinite darkness, blacker than any shade known to man. The endless sky appeared like a mottled watercolor painting, its dark blue light bleeding into the volcanic land below. The air itself was charged with an electric current that stimulated the nerve endings on his flesh, causing his skin to erupt with goosebumps.

He suddenly dropped to the hot, rocky ground and writhed in ecstasy under the gaze of a dozen heavenly spheres, the scarlet satellites looping around the horizon until the sensations brought him to orgasm. He wiped tears of pleasure from his eyes, got back to his feet, and carried onward.

As he trekked further into the dreamscape, the soot at his feet grew hot until the skin on his soles burned and peeled away. His soul was so filled with elation he scantly noticed the pain, nor the faceless souls of those he'd wronged, watching his every step.

Again, he heard the familiar voice, powerful and soothing, as it called to him from beyond the void. The words carried on the howling wind, undecipherable at first, but becoming increasingly clearer as he waded through the dream. "Aurelio," the words echoed repeatedly.

Deep into the dreamscape, Aurelio came upon an ashen man sitting on a marble throne, every inch of his skin covered by swarming flies. The man smiled crookedly, his arching brows shifting a crown of severed fingers atop his head.

"Do you know who I am?" the man said, his voice carrying forcefully across the air.

Aurelio knelt. "You are the Apostle of Bloat. I have heard your voice in my dreams."

The Apostle smiled, flashing a set of yellow teeth embedded inside tar-colored gums. "I've been looking for you for a long time."

The Apostle curled his index finger, beckoning Aurelio forth. "Where do you come from?"

Aurelio shuffled toward the Apostle. The buzzing of the flies grew into an angry frenzy. "I come from a world of grief and death. Of decay and finality."

"I see," said the Apostle. "And what do you seek?"

"I don't have much time before our link is severed," Aurelio pleaded. "Soon, I will awake to a world of sadness. I wish to stay here with you forever in everlasting peace and joy."

The Apostle leaned back in his throne and nodded. "Come closer and I shall impart upon you grand wisdom."

Nervously, Aurelio approached the Apostle. Flies scattered from the king's head, revealing a man who looked eerily like Aurelio, save for his blue, gaunt flesh and the hollowed-out pits where his eyes should have been. Aurelio trembled at the terrible visage before him.

"Do not fear," the Apostle said as the flies settled back on his face. "Your days of running are at an end. A world of love and peace awaits." The Apostle leaned forward, his cracked blue lips nearly touching Aurelio's earlobe. "The way to bridge the gap between worlds is to taste one's own fruit."

Aurelio's own lips quivered. "One's own fruit?"

The Apostle of Bloat stood and placed a hand on Aurelio's shoulder, clamping sharp-nailed fingers into his flesh.

Aurelio jolted awake to the summer heat circulating inside his motel room, the fire of the candles spitting his flickering shadow on the wall. The light of the moon pierced the broken slats on the window, painting his torso blue. His bedsheets stuck to his sodden body, the sweat pungent with the contaminated waste circulating through his blood.

Aurelio's arms shuddered as he sat up against the headboard. He reached for the nightstand and unclipped the box cutter from his jeans.

His glistening belly rose and fell as he labored to breathe, his lungs filling with fluid. The fire in his head had spread through every limb and muscle and every movement felt like a minuscule torture. Aurelio licked his dry lips and dragged the blade across his abdomen, wincing as the wound split open and wept its warm syrup into his lap.

Like fruit.

The bedsheets readily accepted his body's scarlet offering, soaking up the blood like a canvas. His face contorted as he reached inside the gash, his fingers probing past the layers of flesh and fat. A wave of numbing coldness began to sweep through the fibers in his stomach, quenching the flaring pain. Black spots began to fill his vision as the blood stains expanded on the bed. Aurelio fought to keep his eyelids open as his trembling hand pulled out a meaty strand of intestine and brought the piece of himself to his lips. He began to gnaw slowly, his teeth chattering as the taste of warm copper filled his mouth. The juices of life seeped down his gullet and chin, branching off and meeting again on his chest like tributaries flowing into a river.

Once he had his fill, Aurelio settled back into a supine position and shut his eyes. The candle at his side began to flicker out as he awaited his final journey to a world where pain and suffering and ghosts were only things of make-believe.

Skins

The morning was cold and overcast, the few slivers of sunlight that caught on Marlon's body did nothing to warm him in the slightest. He cursed under his balaclava and tried to listen for the sounds of helicopters and schooners over the groan of ice scraping alongside the boat.

They had been far out at sea; farther even than most fishing vessels had typically ventured this time of the season. He doubted anyone had followed them to this empty stretch of coastline; there was nothing out here but pain and emptiness.

Uncle Harrold jumped onto the ice first, wasting no time. When Marlon was certain everything was clear, he cocked his rifle and vaulted over the side of the boat after him.

As he landed, the ice beneath his boots cracked. "Fuck," he whispered. He took a gentle step forward, using the rifle to steady himself like a tightrope walker. The ice shelf had appeared solid from out at sea, but now he wasn't so sure it would hold long beneath his girthy frame.

"Hey, Biggie," Uncle Harrold said, turning back at him. "Get your fat butt over here, kid. I count five seals. If we can corral them into a tight killzone, it'll make our jobs easier."

Marlon nodded and trudged ahead as a fierce gust blew in. The cold began to cut into his hands like a thousand razors. Forgetting his gloves at the docks had been stupid, even for him. He wiggled his fingers to keep the blood pumping, hoping he could still pull off a decent shot when the time came. The last thing he wanted was to screw this up. Hell, he couldn't afford to at this point. He shrugged off the thought and tried to focus. If his uncle was to be believed, he was five well-placed shots away from paying off his bookies.

Apparently, there was a healthy illicit market for seal skins, meat, and blubber outside the watchful jurisdiction of the Canadian government. Sketchy buyers whose identities were best left anonymous. "Put it like this," his uncle had told him, "if it exists, there's a market for it." Uncle Harrold knew all about stuff like that. He got to know some big players during his stint in prison.

Marlon spotted a pair of plump, spotted seal cubs meandering across the ice. Siblings, perhaps. Their eyes glimmered like fresh snowpack in the distance as they bellyflopped playfully over one another on the edge of the shelf. He felt a tug at his heart. He wasn't the kind to do this under ordinary circumstances, but he was in a predicament. A life-and-death sort of bind.

A few bad poker hands could doom a man in extremely horrific ways.

Uncle Harrold brandished what resembled a pickaxe and brought it close to his chest. The club had a small, blunt hammer head on one end, and a long, curving hook on the other.

"What is that thing?" Marlon said raising his voice over the wind's roar.

His uncle stroked his gray beard, keeping his eyes fixed on a solitary seal that had strayed from the pack. "A hakapik," he shouted back. "After you shoot the things in the head, I'll come in close and smash their skulls with one end, and hook their bodies onto the boat with the other. You can guess which side does what."

Marlon felt his insides churn. He was glad he was only going to be doing the shooting. A single well-placed shot meant a quick death. Hell, he wouldn't even be doing the skinning. Still, he couldn't help but feel dirty inside. He tried to change the subject. "What are you gonna do with your share of the money, Uncle Harrold?"

His uncle smiled. "Well, Biggie, I wasn't gonna tell you until later, but I was planning on giving you my cut. I figured you won't have much left after you pay off your debts, and you'll need something to get you back on your feet. I mean, what's family for, am I right?"

Before Marlon could respond, a loud crack filled the air. Uncle Harrold's head exploded in a burst of hair, flesh, and red chunks before his body toppled to the ground. Another explosion. Something struck Marlon's jaw. He fell beside his uncle's corpse where his blood had canvased the ice like a bucket of spilled paint.

Marlon's face flared with pain as he reached for his rifle. Then came another crack, and his right hand blew apart in a burst of bloody fragments.

He howled while his wounds throbbed to the beat of his racing heart. Then came darkness; a few moments in and out of consciousness elapsed before he heard the sound of crunching beside him.

"These two will do," said a gruff voice. "Lots of skin between the both of them. Probably family."

"Mm," said another. "Plenty of nourishment and warmth to be had. The buyers will be pleased."

Marlon managed to turn his head slightly. A hakapik came down on Uncle Harrold's spine, the hook lodging itself deep into his tissue. Streaks of crimson trailed his body as it was dragged across the ice.

In his peripheral, he spotted the twin seal pups slithering off the shelf and into the sea. He thought about crawling for the edge. It couldn't have been more than ten meters away. Through the pain, Marlon inhaled a deep breath, and with his remaining hand, dug his fingers into a crack in the ice shelf and tried to pull himself forward.

As he crawled, his head scraped along the jagged floor, the impact dislodging a few teeth from the cavity in his face.

The crunching of ice reared up in the distance again.

He lay still, crying. Warm tears streamed down his face, burning as they entered his wounds.

"That one's lost a hand," called out the gruff voice.

"Yes."

"Should still fetch a fair price," the gruff voice added. "Lots to work with. Lots of skin."

The cold began to numb Marlon's body as he lay beside a pool of expanding blood. Before he blacked out, he heard the crunching of ice stop behind him. It was then that he was glad he wouldn't feel much before the end.

Shantytown: A Mexican Ghost Story

Maribel pressed her hands to her ears as the rooftop rattled, the sound like pots and pans crashing on the floor. A corner of the tin roof flapped upward revealing a wedge of night sky. She pictured the shadow people skulking above, pulling back the frame as they hunted for someone to devour.

"Mami," she said pulling her bedsheets up to her chin, "the ghosts are back." As if playing on her fears, the curtains on the windows—which were nothing more than holes in the walls—fluttered inward, like phantom feelers grasping for victims.

Her mother moaned. A beam of moonlight pierced the opening in the roof, partially illuminating her in the blackness of the shack. Her cheeks looked sunken in and her ribs protruded where her tank top had rolled up her torso. "It's the wind, mija," she said rolling on her side to face the wall. "There's no such thing as ghosts." Like a string of pearls, the outline of her spine pressed against her brown skin. A skeleton ready to shed its human host.

As the shack trembled and groaned, Maribel wondered, as she always did, if their home had been haunted. Her mother had reassured her that it wasn't. The sounds she'd heard were just the shoddy, rotting bones of the foundation like the creaking of old hinges, the scraping of branches against the roof, and the wind whistling through porous walls. Besides, the dwelling wasn't that old, she'd said, so no one else had lived or died here before.

"What if it's Papi's ghost?" Maribel said watching as the corner of the roof peeled back farther. Five long shadowed fingers slithered down the wall below the open cavity. Her heart thrummed against her chest until it burned. She hoped, at least, that it was only her father's ghost and nothing more.

Her mother grumbled into the wall, her voice low and muffled. "He's not dead, mija. He probably just started a new family across the border."

Just then the roof ceased its fluttering and the shadowed fingers receded. The moonlight gone, the world returned to darkness. Maribel lay still allowing her heart to settle back into place. Her mother's snores took the place of the wind's roar.

The heat soon swelled in the room and she began to sweat like she did when her mother roasted peppers over an open fire in the summer. It didn't take long for her gown to stick to her body like a wet plastic bag.

Nights like this stretched on forever.

She clambered over the bed, careful her clothes didn't catch on the loose springs jutting from the edge of the mattress. She slipped on a pair of chanclas and nudged the door open.

Before she stepped outside, she checked on her mother. Her obscured body rose and fell softly like a sleeping baby.

Across the basin, another gust blew in, the cool catching on the beads of sweat dotting her skin. She closed her eyes and smiled, allowing herself to enjoy the little comforts the night occasionally provided.

Throughout the colonia baja, the sheet metal roofs shuddered, but there were no shadow people prowling along their rusted surfaces. No ghosts, no monsters, nothing out of the ordinary. Besides the breeze's howling, the shantytown had been tranquil this night. Nothing but the familiar cluster of homes built from crates, cinderblocks, corrugated steel, and all the little things one could find floating along the river.

Makeshift towns like this were common throughout Tijuana. Clusters of roughshod dwellings and the poor people who inhabited them. It's all Maribel had known. Before they had moved here, they'd lived in one on the western foothills of the city. When the factories had shuttered there, they'd relocated up north where a horde of new ones had popped up.

At her back the maquiladora sat perched atop the hill, its drain pipes jutting out the side of the cliff. Dark runoff flowed into the dry riverbed, bisecting the town in a river that ran murky and pungent. Some days it smelled acrid and left her choking, others it smelled like dead rats. Mother told her never to drink from it, even on those hot days when her throat was dry and her lips would crack.

The town knew the polluted water came from the American-owned factory, but her mother had told her working there was a blessing because it afforded them food. Not everyone in town was so fortunate. Some settlers were stranded deportees from other countries who couldn't secure asylum or squatters with nowhere else to go.

She hated that her mother worked there from sunrise to sunset. The only time they spent together anymore was in silence at dinner or on her day off as they collected fresh water from the water truck. Maribel wished she were older so she could work at the factory with her mother, but that wouldn't be for some time. She counted with her fingers. Maybe ten more years.

Since she didn't have the luxury of school, Maribel would spend most of the day scribbling on the outer walls of the shack with the worn-down crayons a pastor had gifted her some time ago. On other days, she spent the afternoons in the company of other kids, making up games and telling each other stories. Sometimes the stories involved the monsters they'd seen or the shadow people that lurked on the fringes of town.

Some of the kids had seen them on nights like this when they were hot or bored and strayed too far from their homes. The shadow people were a group of gangly ghosts that prowled the border wall, just past the colonia's edges. And if you spotted them it was a sure bet you'd hear the cries of their victims soon after. Screams of "Ack! Ack! Ack!" as they were chopped to pieces and tossed over the other side of the wall. Some of the kids' parents said that they didn't exist. Others said the shadow people only came for tattletales, so it was best to mind your business and shut up.

Every now and then one of the children would go missing, never to come back. No one ever really knew what had happened, but the rumblings around the colonia said they had run away to seek better lives, or perhaps they'd joined the cartels with the allure of easy money. Maribel knew, though. All the children knew.

She shook the thought and glanced at the dark, endless sky. The stars weren't visible, like most nights. If it weren't for the moonlight, the town would have sat in complete darkness, each shack a tomb in a cemetery. That's what this town really was.

A shiver ran along her neck and arms. Before she turned back inside, shrieks bellowed out over the thicket beyond the northern edge of the colonia. She waited for the adults to come out and investigate but no one did. Had the wind masked the screams as it tore through the trees and bushes? Maybe she had imagined it.

Again, the wails came. She wasn't sure but she thought she heard the words, "Help me," echo across the basin.

Maribel hesitated and took a step forward. Then another. Curiosity and momentum pushed her north along the inky river's path where she thought the sound had come from.

A breeze carried the rancid smell of the stream whipping across her face. She stifled a cough with her hand as she felt her throat begin to burn. She lifted her gown over her nose and stopped suddenly at the exact spot where she'd seen her first monster. How long had it been? She'd lost track a while ago, most nights since having bled into one another like a long, blurry nightmare.

This particular memory was still vivid, though. She and a few other children had been playing that night, jabbing sticks into the river to see what odd things they could fish out. She was the first to spot it wading lazily along the stream. She recalled its bruised pale-blue flesh partially submerged in burbling water, its bulging eyes locked on her, unblinking. Apart from its lolling tongue, what scared her the most was its puffy, tight skin, like a latex glove ready to burst when you blew too much air into it. She screamed. The rest of the children scrambled home in tears.

By the time the adults came to see what had happened the thing was already gone. Flushed away into the void. Her mother had scolded her for making things up and getting everyone so worked up when they were trying to sleep.

She peered away from the river. The dense thicket where she'd heard the screams was not more than twenty yards from where she stood, the border wall not much farther than that. The river flowed past the wall and emptied into an estuary in San Diego. Mother wouldn't let her venture further than the outskirts of the colonia, though. That side was dangerous. Everyone knew that. That was alright by her; out beyond the tree line was where the shadow people were known to dwell.

Despite what her mother had said, Maribel had always known this town was haunted and there were indeed such things as ghosts and monsters. Things moved freely in the dark here when the adults weren't looking. Some nights, it seemed, they inched a little closer.

She thought about the screams again. Had she heard right? Maybe it was a wounded animal. Those were best left alone. *Carrion for the birds*, her mother had said anytime Maribel cried at the sight of an injured kitten on the side of the road. *Keep your head down and worry about yourself.*

40

She wanted to turn back home now. But what if someone really had called out? She couldn't leave without offering help.

She regarded the wilderness ahead and paused, hoping to hear something again. Nothing stirred or chirped or rattled. Hesitant to take another step, she called out where she stood. "Hello? Is anyone there?"

No reply except her echo and the rustling of leaves.

She should have known it was her imagination. She had gotten so worked up over the wind ripping at the roof that the mundane now seemed especially frightening at night. She pivoted to turn home. If she was lucky, her mother still wouldn't have noticed she'd been missing.

A long, grating screech erupted beyond the trees, sending birds darting into the air like black bottle rockets. A pair of glowing yellow eyes emerged from the dark of the thicket. She shielded her face with both hands, the light like needles in her eyes.

For a long while they watched each other, Maribel unable to move her legs no matter how hard she tried to pull away. Time stretched; the moment stuck in agonizing perpetuity. The watcher in the dark didn't move. It only observed as she stood paralyzed, the warm tears streaming down her face. She wanted to cry out for Mami but her mouth wouldn't let her form the words.

Maribel pressed her eyes shut. Her limbs began to tremble. A sliver of moisture ran down her legs, pooling at her feet. She tried to recite the Lord's Prayer but the words wouldn't come. She tried instead to think of her father but couldn't remember his face. Her mind found no comforts to dispel the terror that lay ahead.

She opened her eyes and offered the thing another glance. The watcher squealed again and its fiery yellow eyes sunk behind the thicket. As the thing spun, she saw the broad side of a car drive off into the night. The land grew dark and the bushes and trees swayed softly again.

On the way home she wiped her tears. Maybe not tonight, but it would only be a matter of time before they got to her. She wouldn't say anything to her mother. There'd be no point. Here, ghosts and monsters roamed free in a land that turned a blind eye to them. Maybe this town wasn't satisfied just being haunted. Maybe it was waiting to make ghosts of them all.

Purveyors and Puppets

Once she'd entered the sanctuary of her home and fastened the bolts on the door, Anna pressed her face against the window. The street was empty, save for the throngs of moths hovering over the flickering light of the lamp posts.

She drew the blinds shut. Four months hadn't put enough distance between her and the stalker hellbent on silencing her "liberal howling." The police weren't sure how he'd acquired her address.

Anna ran a hand along the back of her neck, massaging the tightly wound coils of muscle. Her fingers glided toward her throat. She felt the raised scar tissue where the knife had sliced her flesh. A carefully placed elbow to his solar plexus and a short run to the neighbor's house had saved her. Thankful couldn't begin to describe how she'd felt escaping with her life that night.

She poured herself a glass of wine and settled into the couch, flipping through TV channels until she found what she was looking for.

The woman on the screen looked back at her through fiery brown eyes as she waxed poetic about the wave of police brutality disproportionately afflicting people of color. Anna's producers told her that she needed to smile more, that a perceived warmth would draw in more viewers. God knew she needed them. After she got out of the hospital, she had the number one show on TV. For two weeks. But as all ratings eventually did, they had started to slide. She chuckled. No. Her issue wasn't smiling, it was finding out who was lighting the show because she looked like a pale corpse under those lights.

"Join us tomorrow as we invite Councilman Robert Tao to discuss his push toward expanding voting rights in his district, the poorest in the state."

Her mobile rang. Anna nearly fumbled her glass. Restricted number. Again. She let it ring.

"Thank you for tuning in to Liberal Lioness," the TV version of herself said, "I'm your host, Anna Acevedo."

Anna looked at her glass and found herself staring back from a pool of sloshing crimson. Her eyes appeared sunken-in, dark. All those sleepless nights. Maybe it wasn't the lighting but the dread that someone had been watching from the shadows. Another fanatic who didn't take kindly to immigrant TV show hosts.

The phone rang again.

Screw it, she thought and picked up.

"Hello, Ms. Acevedo?" a soft-spoken woman on the line said.

"I'm sorry, who is this?" Anna downed the wine.

"Sorry to call so late. My name is Dakota Ellsworth, I'm a producer on *The Daily Roundup* with Kirk Sullivan."

"That right-wing asshole?"

"Correct," Ellsworth said.

"Why are you calling me?" Anna said, wondering how they'd gotten her number.

"We'd like to invite you onto the show tomorrow evening. We know it's last minute but Mr. Sullivan has requested your appearance. He values your opinions."

"Bullshit," Anna said. "He's been taking shots at me since I premiered last year. Some of his viewers have taken his message to heart, as I'm sure you know." She swore she could feel the scar on her throat begin to throb.

"Network chest-puffing. Spectacle. Grabbing for ratings, as you know. He personally finds your point of view refreshing and engaging. He even admires your story. Immigrant who made her own way in this country? Nothing short of the American Dream."

Anna didn't respond.

"You'll be compensated," Ellsworth said. "And it'll be a fair discussion. Our show boasts the highest evening news ratings so your appearance could offer your own program a boost."

Ellsworth wasn't wrong. Critics, bloggers, die-hard liberals; they'd all tune in just to see what the fuss was about. Higher ratings meant a longer contract and a larger platform. And it just so happened her contract was almost up. After a long pause she sighed and said, "Ok, I'll do it."

"Wonderful," Ellsworth said. She filled Anna in on the details and thanked her for her time.

What would her producers think? That she was being led into an ambush, surely. *Damn.* But would they also think it was worth the risk?

Anna put her hand over her eyes. She'd been so tired she forgot to ask what they'd be discussing. A woman's right to complete bodily autonomy? Or perhaps immigration and the influx of "parasites" infiltrating the country? Either way she'd come prepared. There was no topic she wouldn't be able to touch by tomorrow night.

Anna flipped on the evening's rerun of *The Daily Roundup* on Avalon News Network. Kirk Sullivan pounded a fist on his desk. The old man was going on another fascist diatribe about government spending and liberal idealogues rotting away traditional values.

Old or not, he looked great under those lights.

The ANN building was dull and inconspicuous; nothing but a big concrete slab and bleak, obsidian windows. Outside, a short, slim blonde held the door open as Anna approached.

"Ms. Acevedo!" she said, smiling warmly while offering her hand.

Anna shook it and smiled back. "Dakota Ellsworth?"

"Yes," she said. "I'm so glad you made it. Please come in." She was younger than Anna had expected, her rosy face radiating the enthusiasm of a college student at her first internship.

Cold air nipped at Anna's arms as she entered the lobby.

"A bit chilly in here," Anna said.

"Hm? Oh, yes," Ellsworth replied. "Sorry about that. Something wrong with the air conditioning. We're working on it."

Ellsworth led her up an old lift and into her green room on the tenth floor.

"We'll send someone over to take care of your makeup in just a moment, we're just prepping the set. Mr. Sullivan is so eager to meet you!"

"Thank you so much," Anna said, taking a seat in front of the mirror. "I'm looking forward to our discussion."

Ellsworth shut the door softly on her way out. She was perky, enthusiastic. Anna knew the type. She remembered those early days out of college having to work twice as hard as everyone else just to land any network gig she could, even if it meant kissing ass.

Immigrant women like herself were seldom taken seriously in the world of political journalism. They were seen as angry, and ill-educated. Exotic eye candy at the most if they fixed themselves up enough.

She balled her hands into fists thinking about it. "This was a mistake," she muttered under her breath. "Sullivan was just going to feed me to the wolves." Anna heard her producer's retort in her head: *Yeah, but wolves are good for ratings.*

Looking up, she caught her tired reflection staring back. The crow's feet along her eyes had begun to carve their way outward like a dry riverbed. The stress of hosting her own show while avoiding murderous zealots was taking its toll on her body, her youth. She smiled. The makeup department had their work cut out for them.

She decided to let her producers know she was getting ready to tape. They'd been ecstatic when she broke the news, told her this was a golden opportunity. She had scoffed. Her show had been hot for a few months. Big deal. The way she saw it she was just a flavor of the month. She needed a ratings spike to keep the momentum going, yes, but doing something like this? But, as always, her producers wanted a little controversy to keep things fresh. She'd learned the hard way that in showbusiness sometimes people needed adversaries, real or imagined, to get things moving. It was too late to back out now.

She unlocked her phone. No reception. *Damn.*

A cold draft blew along her skin, turning her hairs prickly. She wrapped her arms across her chest and looked around but couldn't find a thermostat in the room. Why was it so damn cold? She crossed the room and peered out the door, hoping to spot a handyman or crewmember who could adjust the settings.

Nothing but a cramped, empty hallway. Curious that no one had been shuffling around; every backstage production she'd ever worked on had been a chaotic affair. Before she returned to the greenroom, she heard glass breaking in the distance.

"Hello?" she asked aloud. "Is everything okay out there?"

No response.

She shrugged and continued down the hall to check on the noise. It would give her an excuse to scope out the behind-the-scenes action at Avalon.

Anna wound through a maze of dingy, tight corridors, the paint on every wall peeling and flaking like the skin on charred corpses. She came upon a large loading area. Overhead, perched on a catwalk, she saw a smoldering ashtray. Someone had recently been here.

From below, she followed the catwalk's path through a dark, open room littered with crates and folding chairs. A pile of glass had been neatly swept into a dustpan.

The sounds of subtle rustling could be heard in the distance. There were voices. Lots of them. Excited, frantic, buzzing. She spotted a long curtain, turned around the bend, and found herself gazing upon *The Daily Roundup* set. And there under the bright lights sat good ol' boy Kirk Sullivan, waiting patiently as a frenzy of crewmembers powdered his pale, wrinkled face.

Anna thought about introducing herself but decided to let the man get done up first. They were probably waiting for her back in the green room, anyway.

She pivoted to turn back when a small light glimmered in her peripheral vision. On the catwalk just above Sullivan's desk, a man unspooled multiple strands of thin fishing wire down to another crewmember who tied the lines around Sullivan's arms, hands, and fingers. The man on the rafters pulled on the wire, lifting Sullivan's limbs like a marionette.

Sullivan's chair rolled backward, revealing a legless torso. Beneath the desk a crewmember stuffed his arm up through a cavity under Sullivan's belly, manipulating his head and jaw like a sock puppet.

Anna stifled a gasp with her hand as her guts twisted themselves into knots. She fought the urge to throw up, pushing down the surge of hot bile in her throat. A flood of tears streamed down her face, dripping off her chin and onto the floor.

"Alright," a tall worker in a red cap said, "hit him with some formaldehyde."

A woman approached Sullivan and jabbed his cheek with a syringe.

"And crank up the AC!" the tall man said. "His skin is looking a little mushy."

Sullivan whipped his head toward Anna. Her heart skipped a beat.

"Hello, Ms. Acevedo," Sullivan said, his lips not in perfect synchronicity with his words. Or had it been the words of his handler beneath the desk? "Am I pronouncing that right? Ah-say-vay-doh?"

She took a step back the way she came and felt an arm wrap around her waist. Then came the sting of a needle at her neck.

There was only a flicker of lightheadedness before the darkness.

Anna wove in and out of consciousness, surrounded by strange men in the cramped interior of the green room. She'd been lying on the loveseat from what she could tell.

She struggled to keep her eyelids open as her head pounded. She felt drowsy, weak. Men wearing latex gloves, many of them brandishing saws and scalpels, pinned her arms down. If she hadn't been so drugged, she would have screamed and cried and kicked. As it was, she couldn't move her legs. Her legs!

She craned her neck as far as she could and peered down the length of her body. Her legs were gone. All that remained of her existed just above the waist. Someone slid a bucket under her torso. Her heart began to race and she turned away toward the ceiling, gasping for air like a dying fish.

Dakota Ellsworth stepped into view and caressed Anna's face with cold fingers. "It's best if you don't look," she said in her soft voice.

Anna tried to speak but her throat was dry and scratchy and the only thing her lips could do were quiver.

"Don't worry, you'll look better than ever when we're all done. I promise." Ellsworth gently squeezed Anna's hand.

Anna squeezed back as hard as her muscles would let her. She licked her lips and mouthed, "Why?"

"The experiment was a failure," Ellsworth said, tracing her fingers along Anna's face in small circles. Ellsworth grimaced while pinching her own face, as if feeling some foreign growth. Her skin stretched out as if it were going to snap apart. "Existence is an infirmity. Consciousness, a malady. We realize that now. Life must be turned on itself. But there are so few of us left," she sighed, her eyes scanning the ceiling like someone gazing deeply at the stars. Stars that weren't there. Her words were mad, but Anna saw something in Ellsworth's gaze. Not madness, but startling clarity.

"We sow malice, hate, lies, and paranoia until it boils to the surface. Then our viewers do the rest and act on that hatred. Like good little puppets. You, yourself, have a built-in viewership that hangs on your every word, frothing at the mouth to act on a political enemy that threatens their perceived way of life. You'll make an excellent addition to the show."

Ellsworth nodded and another woman approached Anna, quickly applying foundation to her face. Next, Anna felt a slight pressure on her belly and heard the wet, sloshing sounds of things dropping into the bucket. There was no pain before darkness came for her again.

47

The red light above the camera blinked on and Kirk Sullivan smiled.

"My next guest is the self-appointed Liberal Lioness, Anna Acevedo. Welcome and thank you for joining us on the show tonight."

Through unseen machinations, Anna's head turned toward the camera and at the millions of viewers at home waiting for blood to spill. The lighting captured her flawless complexion and fiery brown eyes perfectly.

She smiled. "It's my pleasure to be here, Kirk."

Roots in Kon Tum

The fisherman offered his passenger an inquisitive look as the boat shuddered along the banks of the river. Frank Reynosa opened his rucksack and fumbled through a few dog-eared photographs until he found what he was looking for.

He'd snuck his camera on most patrols back then, snapping pictures of anything that caught his eye. This picture in particular had washed out over the years, but he could still make it out as it shook in his hand. In it, dozens of dead and dying American and NVA troops lay spilled out over the banks of the Sesan River, their blood seeping into the water and soil.

He turned away from the photograph and looked upon the same river as it wound lazily through the countryside in Kon Tum Province. It was almost exactly as he remembered it, save for the dead, gnarled trees hanging over the water.

Frank nodded and the fisherman rowed the boat to a stop. He paid the man and humped it over a small slope. On the other side, what he remembered to be a sprawling jungle had now been reduced to nothing but a barren swath of black, rotting trees, their branches twisting into odd forms like the limbs of a contortionist. He remembered that day in 1967 when Company C had been ambushed by North Vietnamese regulars using the very same trees as cover.

He tracked over dead soil, dark and gritty like ground charcoal. He thought he felt minute vibrations in the ground as if the dirt was sifting under his boots. What had happened here? It had all been so beautiful once. Even fifty plus years ago, when it had been littered with arms and legs, and half-blown men, gasping like dying fish, he never forgot how green it all was, how lush. Like fools playing war in the Garden of Eden.

He scanned the ground for signs of hollow ditches, mass graves, anything, but it was pointless. It had been so long. The NVA had forced them into a full retreat, the dead and wounded left behind. He'd been lucky to get out intact, let alone start a family and see his grandkids make it through college. A certain guilt had gnawed at his insides over the years, but it wasn't survivor's guilt. It had been something else, entirely. Frank shook away the thought and hiked ahead.

A few miles north, the village remained unchanged. A few thatched huts huddled together alongside some concrete and corrugated metal shacks, little more than a farming commune.

Storm clouds began to gather, casting the village in a web of shadows. He pulled his jacket in tight and strolled past a few chickens and some antique Fords idling on narrow dirt roads. A man as old as himself, withered and wrinkled, smoked a cigarette against the wall of a hootch and watched him in silence. Frank approached the man. "Hello. Xin chào. My name is Frank Reynosa. I was in your country many years ago. During the war."

"Yes," the man said, nodding.

"I lost many friends not too far from here. As I'm sure you did. A battle near the river. Do you know what became of the bodies? A grave or a memorial, perhaps, where I could pay my respects?"

"The earth swallowed them all," the man said, smiling through brown teeth. "The trees grew a taste for blood."

Frank smiled. "Right. Listen, the reason I'm here." He pulled an old photograph from his jacket pocket and held it up in front of him. "Do you happen to know this woman?"

The old man scanned the picture, a faded sepia portrait of a young Vietnamese woman flashing a shy smile, her hair draped over her face, partly covering one of her eyes. The man's gaze settled back on Frank in a look of disgust before he turned away.

On the opposite side of town, a handful of farmers toiled over a small rice paddy. Beyond the paddies, tracts of dead land extended to the base of a mountain on the horizon, the dead trees encircling the village like sentries. He flagged an old woman near the edge of the field.

She sauntered over and offered a warm smile. "Hello," she said.

"Hello, yes," he said. "My name is Frank Reynosa. I was hoping you could help me with something." He handed the woman the same photograph he'd shown the man before. "I patrolled this village many years ago during the war. During my few weeks here, I met the woman in this photograph, and we became friendly. She became pregnant. And, well, I'm here to try to correct my mistakes while I still have time."

Tears streamed from the woman's eyes. She covered her mouth to muffle her sobs. She took Frank's hand and led him toward the outskirts of town where a long straw hut sat beside itself in the shadows of the clouds.

Inside, a group of young men sat around a table playing poker as a small radio played some old Chuck Berry tunes. Some men had missing arms, others nursed cleft palates. One man dealt the cards with webbed hands. Further in, a few children slept on cots while exposed sections of their spines protruded from their lower backs. People without eyes ambled about, the voices of their loved ones guiding them toward rotting chairs.

"After the battle," the woman said, "your airplanes spray chemicals to kill our trees and crops so North Vietnamese could not hide or eat. Chemicals change everything. People. The land. Our children and grandchildren pay the price today. Cannot leave. No one leaves."

"Agent Orange," Frank said as his heart sank into his bowels. "Dioxin." He ran a hand through his gray hair. He felt their stares on him. Even the blind ones could breathe in the stink of his guilt. What had the Army done to them? It was hard to digest, seeing these people wallowing on the fringes, outcasts even in their own village.

Outside, rain began to pelt the ground.

"The girl in the picture," the old woman said, "was my sister Mai. She passed many years ago." She waved a hand toward another room. It was dark, Frank couldn't make out anything inside. A few thunderous snores emanated from within and nothing more. "Your children and grandchildren are in there. Would you like to meet them?"

Frank stepped back. What would he find in there? Would they be limbless? Just trunks of meat who'd call him Daddy? Or would their spines extend from their backs like reptilian tails? The thought of eyeless, disfigured strangers reaching out to embrace him made his skin crawl. He placed a hand over his mouth, fighting the urge to wretch on the floor. "No, I better not. I've made a mistake."

He turned and ran back as fast as his old legs would let him, slogging through the mud. The sludge was thick, like tar, as it pulled on his boots with every step.

By the time he found the tree line near the riverbank, his lungs were on fire. He stopped to lean against a tree. It was a mistake to come back. What did he think he'd find? He couldn't bring any of what he'd seen back home. What would his family say? His *real* family. Sometimes it was best to let the past have its funeral.

Frank mustered on as a tempest fell violently, raindrops stinging his face like needles. Before he reached the edge of the slope, his boot caught on a dead root. He slammed face-first into the mud, where a skull washed past his face. The unbearable smell of rot wafted across the air, stinging his eyes. In revolt, he jerked his head away. As the rains fell, femurs and scapulae and hip bones rose to the surface, like bubbles in a boiling soup.

"Oh, fuck!" Frank said, scrambling to push himself up, but his hands only sunk further into the earth. He cursed, feeling his hot breath bounce off the ground. Springing from the mud like snakes, a slew of dead, thorny roots pierced his flesh and coiled around his limbs and rucksack, pulling him deeper into the muck.

He wanted to call for help. Maybe the boatman was still on the other side. He opened his lips, but a thin, jagged shoot lanced down his throat, muting his scream. The roots tightened their grasp on his body until he was spilling blood into the mud.

As the roots pulled him deeper into the filth, he thought he saw the faces of his brothers from Company C, the NVA infantrymen, even those of his family. But as the earth sapped him of every last drop, he realized the only thing waiting to greet him was the darkness.

Midnight Frequencies

The streetlight buzzed above the taco truck like a nest of angry hornets as it flickered in its death throes. Like most neglected corners in Los Angeles, this particular stretch of downtown had been left to the bottom-feeders. At least down here, Enrique thought, the cops didn't harass street vendors all that much.

"Here you go, brother," Enrique said, sliding the order of carne asada fries across the service counter.

"Thanks, Rick," Mike said, jabbing the plastic fork into the mound of steaming fries. The drunkard's shadow danced manically on the sidewalk as the streetlight offered a final flicker before burning out. Under the concession window's pale blue light, Mike's face looked lifeless, cold. Like a living corpse. "I'll see you next week, amigo." The man stumbled down the street until his footfalls became whispers and the night absorbed his body.

Enrique ducked his head under the window and peered out into the night. Like twisted flecks of light, the stars above became distorted in a haze of light pollution. A few shooting stars streaked to Earth before fading from view. He smirked and made a wish.

Not far off from the truck, the skyscrapers blotted out the moon shrouding everything below in a latticework of darkness. Apart from a few vagrants taking refuge in the shadowed nooks of shuttered businesses, the streets were empty.

Enrique crinkled his nose. The air was thick with summer's heat, pungent with the smell of motor oil, urine, and the rot of discarded food scattering the ground.

Before he turned back, he spotted movement in the corner of his eye. Just beside the back tire and under the shadow of a flipped paper plate, he saw maggots hard at work on a half-eaten taco. His eyes followed a trail of gore, where in the alcove of a storm drain, the bugs had gotten to feasting on a lifeless rat's burst intestines. An ecosystem unto itself, the streets truly were the empire of the bottom-feeder.

He turned from the gnarly curbside banquet and shuffled toward the front of the truck, fidgeting with the knob on his police scanner. He'd haggled the janky thing off some screwball Vietnam vet at a flea market rambling about government cover-ups. There were things, the man had alleged, going on all the time. All one had to do was tune in to the right frequency and listen.

Enrique thought the scanner would be a good investment to help keep tabs on police activity, though besides the constant hum of the generator, it had been quiet tonight. No screams, no gunshots. The usual reports of drunk and disorderly conduct had been unusually low, as had reports of assaults or rapes or even calls to shut down street vendors. It was his kind of night.

At the moment, a dispatcher was squawking into the radio about a possible nude male harassing a couple of folks two blocks from his location. Working downtown had exposed him to a different environment. A hidden world most people didn't get to experience from the comfort of their homes. A world of filthy, violent things and transgressions not normally seen in decent society. He thought he'd steeled himself to that kind of stuff but, he couldn't help feeling a shiver run up the back of his neck just thinking about it.

Enrique switched off the burners. The bins had been nearly emptied of carnitas, lengua, and adobada. Not too shabby for a Thursday night. He peeked inside the cashbox. It would be enough to make rent this week with a little extra left over for the child support. It was honest, hard work, and it was starting to pay off.

His moment of pride was shattered as a police siren wailed in the distance.

"No," he muttered under his breath. "Not now."

For a moment Enrique felt his chest tighten. He didn't have a permit and couldn't handle another stint in prison. After he'd done his time, he'd struggled to secure a loan to buy the truck. Now that he had, he couldn't afford to lose his business. His kids were counting on him. Without the money, Stefanie wouldn't be able to make ends meet and they'd all be out in the street in a month's time.

The truck suddenly rocked as the patrol car zipped down the street. Its blaring sirens faded as the car cut a hard corner, disappearing deep into the bowels of downtown.

Enrique sighed and wiped the sweat from his brow with the back of his hand. He shook off the panic and got to scraping the griddle clean. After he wiped down the residue with a wet cloth, he covered the bins in aluminum foil. When he finished, he opened a bottle of Mexican Coke and leaned against the counter.

He drew a heavy sigh. Sometimes he could still see their faces contorted on the asphalt. Their features were blurred, but the streaming crimson puddles pooling under their heads were still vibrant, shimmering under his headlights near the divider. Once he'd expunged the intoxication from his body, the years in prison brought even clearer memories. But he knew better now. He was on a different path. Honest to God.

When he was halfway done with the bottle, the scanner crackled and whined, piercing his eardrums like daggers.

"Fuck!" He twisted the dial and tuned to a different frequency. There was silence for a moment before he heard what sounded like wet, sloshing noises. Almost like the squirmy sounds when someone stirs mac n' cheese.

Ssssssss. The radio crackled back to life.

Then, soft, guttural voices began to slither in between those long moments of scrambled interference.

"Made." *Ssss.* "Planetfall," said one voice in broken English. "Have acquired language."

"Yes," replied another voice. "Language."

"Tonight." *Sssss.* "We. Consume."

"Yes," said the second speaker. "Consume. Need meat."

The radio shrieked, a shrill sound like metal scraping against metal. Another voice. Deeper. "Hunger." *Sssss.* "Meat. Meat. Meat."

Something rapped on the counter. Enrique spun around, his heart nearly bursting out of his chest. "Jesus Christ, Willy, you fucking scared me."

Willy rubbed his frizzled chin and flashed a near-toothless grin. The homeless man had poked his head halfway inside the truck. "Aw, I'm sorry, Rick. Just wanted to ask if you could hook me up with a taco or two."

"Sure thing, brother." Enrique turned on the burner. "Carnitas okay?"

"Anything you can spare, my good man."

Enrique chopped up some roast pork and slapped it on the griddle. When it was done, he shoved the meat in between two pairs of tortillas, gave it a pinch of onion and cilantro, and squeezed on some red salsa from a squirt bottle.

"Here you go, Willy." Enrique slid him the paper plate, smiling. "Try to stay out of trouble."

Willy nodded. He tilted his head back and inhaled the aroma of hot pork. "Thank you, hermano and God bless." The man shuffled toward a sheltered spot under the awning of a wholesale jewelry store and got to munching.

"Just trying to earn my soul back," Enrique said to himself. He wondered if he hadn't been too late.

A scraping sound echoed at his back. Out of the driver side window he spotted a pair of men across the street lurking in the darkness between the streetlights, their heads stooped, hands stuffed inside their jacket pockets. They stood there, still and silent. Pair of hoodlums, he assumed.

Enrique squinted his eyes. He could almost swear their shadowed faces were moving, scrambling like the static on those old analog TV sets he remembered from his childhood. After knocking back the rest of his Coke, he shook his head. Fuck. It had been a long night and home was calling. Time to wrap things up.

He shoved his hands under the cold, running water from the sink and thought about the kids as he scrubbed. He'd been on speaking terms with their mother again. Things were looking up with the business and he found himself smiling as he placed the food into the cooler. He closed his eyes and allowed himself to think of the possibilities. A new car. An apartment in a better part of town. A permit, so he could sell to gringos outside of Laker games. That's where the money was at.

The scanner came alive again with a jarring hiss.

"Man in truck," screeched one voice.

"Yes." *Ssss.* "Man in truck," said another.

"Man in truck. Man in truck. Man in truck. Man in truck."

Sssssssss.

Enrique glanced out the window again. A few more men stepped out of the alley, hands in their pockets, their gazes fixed on his truck. Shit. It wasn't unusual to have some wise guys try to shake him loose of change from time to time. His hand slid toward the switchblade hanging on his belt.

There was scraping behind him now, like shoes kicking up pebbles. When Enrique turned, he spotted a tall, slender man hobbling in from the shadows, another drunkard looking to satisfy his midnight cravings. As the man stepped into the concession window's cone of blue light, Enrique could see his—*its*—complexion clearly. An orgy of squirming maggot-like insects composed the vague shape of a pallid head, their wriggling masses etching raised lips across the thing that was its face. The maggots had even hollowed out small, dark pits for eyes. Lifeless, yet all-seeing eyes.

The thing turned to Enrique and smiled. Its upper set of "teeth" chomped down on its bottom lip which then squirted out white pus-like fluid, as some maggots were undoubtedly pressed to death. The maggot-thing was dressed in dirty rags: nothing but a hoodie and gray sweats. Hanging at its side, its slimy hand gripped a police radio caked with blood.

Its lips shifted awkwardly before they puckered. A thin, grayish tongue pressed against the roof of its mouth as it spoke. "Come. From. Far. Away," it said with a grating voice. "What is… best meat?"

"I-I don't know what you mean," Enrique, said, backing into the wall. The window would be too small for him to crawl out of. He unhooked the knife from his belt, but his fingers became thin, clumsy things and he dropped it on the floor. The meat cleaver lay just out of reach beside the griddle.

What felt like a hot coal began to bore through his chest. What the fuck was happening? This… this couldn't be real. He crossed himself and recited the Lord's Prayer in his head as he had in prison during those long, arduous years.

The maggot-thing ducked under the raised concession flap, a slew of flies hovering around its body. "What is… best meat?" It said again, its breath hot and smelling of decay and death. The thing's hands clutched the counter and maggots spilled everywhere, their writhing bodies making the same wet noises he'd heard on the radio.

Enrique, shivering now, stifled a sob with the crook of his elbow. The warm tears pooling under his eyes began to sting.

The maggot-thing leaned its head inside the window and flicked its tongue out as it tasted the warm air around it. "Best. Meat."

Enrique raised a trembling hand and pointed to that dark spot under the awning where Willy had now fallen asleep. He lay there huddled into a ball atop a cardboard mattress.

The maggot-thing turned toward Willy, snoring in the shadows, and raised its radio to its mouth. "Meat. Acquired."

The group of shrouded figures stumbled across the street. Their radios crackled as they ambled past the truck, a constant static like meat sizzling on a grill.

Willy, in his slumber, lay oblivious to the half-dozen terrors as they approached him.

Enrique jumped in the driver's seat, turned the ignition, and sped off, shoving the guilt way down where he'd never be able to find it. Just as he always had.

He shut off the police scanner as he heard Willy's anguished shrieks. From the rearview mirror he watched as the skyline shrunk and faded behind him. Tomorrow night, Enrique told himself, he'd ditch the scanner and find a new spot in town.

The Cellar

Ramona opened her eyes and the world had gone to hell. The sprawl of farmland—the verdant pastures, the golden rolling hills—had become engulfed in flames. Andres had been shaking her by her shoulders, and, though his lips were moving, the sound of his voice had been drowned out by the roar of the wildfire outside.

Slowly, the words became audible. "We've gotta go. Start the car!"

Her hands trembled as they turned the key in the ignition. When the engine rumbled to life, she pulled out of the shoulder and peeled down the road.

How long had they nodded off? She remembered the motel. There'd been no vacancy and she'd been exhausted. Andres wasn't legally allowed to drive so they had no choice but to sleep on the side of the road. *It's only for a night*, her brother had said in response to her protests.

And now…

Fierce gales whipped across the fields, the embers of burning crops flickering out in the starless night sky. Ramona looked for road signs but the air was choked with smoke and dust and ash. The beams of her headlights seldom cut more than a few feet through that haze. Like driving through a ghostly veil.

"I can't see a thing," Ramona said, squinting her eyes, easing up on the gas. "I don't know where we are."

Andres checked his flip phone but it was dead. He turned on the dome light, pulled an old road atlas from the glove compartment, and unfolded it over his lap.

"Last I remember," he said tracing a finger over folds in the creased paper, "we were on the Five before we turned east onto the One-Ninety-Eight. I think we're somewhere in Huron."

That's right. Fresno County. A small farming town in California's lush Central Valley. They were on their way to see their uncle Ramon, who'd generously offered Andres a job at his farm now that he was out of prison. Something to get him back on his feet.

She glanced at the rearview mirror. "Shit." The world was awash in orange light. "I don't know that we can get out of this."

"Wait," Andres said, pointing to something on the side of the road. "What's that? Is that a tractor?"

An old, rusted combine sat at the mouth of a small path that cut inland. The fires had yet to burn through the fields ahead. Maybe there was a farmstead up that way, someone with a phone.

Ramona considered her options, found she had none, and turned up the trail. The car rolled along a dirt road, past a pair of tractors, a dried up well, and some antiquated booster pumps. Swaths of broken stalks jutted from dead soil. The land hadn't been used for farming in quite some time.

The road terminated in front of a derelict farmstead, the clapboards dilapidated, its ceiling collapsed. A silo and barn sat in shambles nearby, razed ruins from another age.

She parked under an acacia tree and gritted her teeth. "Damn," she said, slamming her hands on the steering wheel. "No one's lived here for years."

"Well, we can't fucking stay here," Andres said, gazing upon the encroaching orange glow.

She thought about reversing, speeding down the road until they'd cleared the fire, but she'd be driving blind through that inferno.

"I need to think," Ramona said, her voice cracking.

A gust blew a sheet of paper against the windshield, obscuring her view. Ramona lowered her window, snatched the paper between her fingers, and pulled it inside the car. The sheet was wrinkled and pulpy and appeared to have been torn from a book. Under the dim glow of the overhead light, she could make out the words *English Grammar and Composition*. The faded words *this book is the property of: Leonela McCoy* were stamped just below that.

"What is that?" Andres said.

Ramona shrugged and flipped the paper over. An elaborate map had been sketched over a blank page in squiggles of red crayon. The map bore a crude illustration of a house and a storm cellar located in the rear. Beside the drawing of the house were the words: *Gateway to the Realm of Fantastika.*

"Come on," Andres said. "We gotta get moving. The fires are spreading."

"Wait," Ramona said. "This map's saying there's a storm cellar behind the house."

"Why the hell would there be a storm cellar?" Andres said. "We're in California. There's no tornados here."

"Let's just check it out," Ramona said, opening the door. "Maybe we can take shelter there. Hope the fires pass us by. It's all we've got."

Andres grimaced before scooting out of the car.

Outside, Ramona felt the heat baking her arms and face, stinging her eyes. Her first instinct was to shield her face in the crook of her arm, to turn away, but there was nowhere *to* turn. Then, a tickle formed in her throat. She began to cough and hack. The smell of wood and smoke became unbearable as cinders rained down on them like snowfall. She lifted her shirt over her nose and jogged around the broad side of the house with its broken windows and graffitied wall.

They found the cellar around the back, its doors obscured by spiderwebs and tangles of thorny overgrowth. Andres parted the weeds. A rusted padlock secured a pair of doors shut. He chambered a kick and brought down his heel, splitting the lock open.

When he swung the doors wide, an abyss of black stared back. Ramona pulled out her phone and waved a light inside but she could scarcely see anything except the vaguest hint of steps descending into that abyss.

She considered the blaze in the distance. In about half an hour, maybe less, it would sweep down on them. She could chance the roads but for all she knew they'd already been enveloped. The smoke would asphyxiate them out there. Here, maybe the subterranean foundation could provide some shelter, buy them time as the fire department battled the blazes, looked for survivors.

Or it could swallow them whole.

"We're going in," Ramona said, rolling up the map, stuffing it into her back pocket.

"No fucking way. It's a death trap in there."

"Listen. Mami and Papi are gone. So is..." She shook her head. "Look, I have to watch out for you, you understand? And I say we're going inside. We have no other choice."

Before he could speak, Ramona grabbed her brother's wrist and led him down the steps. Andres sighed and shut the cellar doors behind them. The black enveloped them like a cloak. In that darkness, something seemed to shift. As if the walls were squirming.

She winced. The smell of sulfur permeated the air. Her eyes felt heavy and her head began to pound. She reached for a guardrail to steady herself but found none.

She took a single, measured step down. Then another. Her shoes became sticky. She aimed the phone's light downward. Her shoes had been coated in a viscous, tar-like substance.

"What the hell is this?" Andres said, lifting a foot. The bottom of his shoes had been covered in the same sludge.

"I don't know. But we gotta keep moving."

With each pace, the steps moaned as they bowed under their weight.

"I think we should go back," Andres said.

Ramona turned to say something but the planks splintered, and they fell into darkness.

They awoke inside of what appeared to be a small cave. The spears of waning sunlight that pierced its entrance kept the darkness behind them at bay. Andres was already standing over her, his hand extended.

Ramona grasped it and pulled herself up. "Where are we?" she said, shielding her eyes as they adjusted to the light.

"I have no idea. But you *have* to see this."

Outside, a magenta cobblestone road began at the mouth of the cave and cut across an expanse of green pastures that stretched toward a horizon capped by rolling hills. The silhouette of a castle overlooked the fields in the distance.

"It's like the Wizard of Oz," Ramona said.

"Huh?"

"The movie," she said. "With the yellow brick road?"

"Never seen it."

Her younger brother never was much of a cinephile. He was, however, apt to roving the streets, drinking, getting into trouble with Armando…

Ramona felt a pang in her guts, a needling in her heart. But now wasn't the time to dwell on the past. They needed to find help. She shoved the pain somewhere deep and looked around. Long, broken clouds streaked across a bright pink sky, like striations of oil color scraped across a canvas by a painting knife. The colors seemed extremely vibrant. Unreal, almost.

"Cotton candy skies," Andres said, nodding at the sky. "Like Papi used to say at Dodger games when the sun was going down."

Ramona shook her head. "How did we get here?"

Andres shrugged. "Hell, if I know."

"Hold on." Ramona pulled the paper from her back pocket and unrolled it. The top of the map had an illustration of twinkling stars and a plunging meteor with a tail of black whipping tendrils in its wake. Below that was the farmhouse and the cellar.

"Gateway to the Realm of Fantastika," she said. "According to this map, we're in some kind of fantasy land." She said it half-jokingly. Truth was, she had no idea why she'd been consulting a map clearly drawn by a child. She supposed because it was all she had to go on.

"A what?" Andres said, leaning in to look at the map.

"Like a land of make-believe. Never mind."

She continued to scan the map. Beneath the picture of the cellar was a landmass divided by various borders which were speckled with cities marked by peculiar names like *Imajynum* and *Lucidium*. She pinpointed the entrance to a cave and jabbed it with her finger. According to the map, they were in a small province called *Krell's Maw*. Local landmarks consisted of the *Well of Wishes*, the *Palace of Peace*, and the *Garden of Dreams*.

"Oh, what's this?" Ramona noticed what appeared to be a note scrawled at the bottom of the page. *This world is not...* but the words ended abruptly as the last segment had been torn off. She must not have noticed. "Shit," she said, under her breath. "I guess we just have to keep moving. The important thing is we're safe. I'm sure we can flag someone down."

Andres stuffed his hands in his jacket and surveyed the new colorful land laid out before him. "Where do we go?"

She nodded toward the path. "We follow the magenta cobblestone road."

They strode along the road for what seemed like a couple of miles. At least forty minutes' worth of walking. But night never came. The same bright pink sky remained fixed above them, unwavering in its rosy brilliance.

She turned to Andres. His four years in the State Penitentiary had aged him. The frown lines and the hints of white hair speckling his stubble spoke of grueling days, of a youth stolen. They hadn't found the time to chat since she'd picked him up. A part of her wanted to ask him how he'd been, how life had treated him. Though, she wasn't sure she was ready to dig around and open those wounds just yet. So, they walked in silence.

The path wound through a thicket. On the other side of the tree line, they found themselves overlooking a garden decorated with rose bushes, tulips, marigolds, and an expansive hedge maze. Ramona consulted the map.

"The Garden of Dreams," she said. "Whatever that means."

The air here smelled sweet and piney with a hint of peppermint and cinnamon. Like the cabin in the mountains during Christmas family vacations when Mami would bake cookies and make champurrado.

Ivy crept along the outer stone walls of a stately palace not too far in the distance.

"And that must be the Palace of Peace," Ramona said.

"Hey," Andres said. "How did those people get here?"

Ramona followed his gaze. A half dozen people lounged around a fountain toward the center of the garden, their murmured conversations distorted by the hum of burbling water. The people vaguely resembled old neighbors from around the block from their childhood in East L.A. Kids from school who had joined gangs. People who had passed on long ago. But she hadn't noticed them when they'd wandered into the garden. They just sort of…appeared.

A dog began to bark nearby. Muffled at first, the barking grew louder, closer. Then, as if out of thin air, a dog appeared before her. Ramona gasped. Max, the family's old golden retriever sprang into her arms.

"Max!" she said, dropping to her knees.

Max pounced on her, smothering her with kisses, his tail flailing. She wrapped her arms around him, touching her head gently to his. Oddly, he felt neither warm nor cold. Her hand moved up his neck, ruffling his mane until her fingers glanced upon the laceration entrenched around his neck.

She let go. How was this possible? The memory was still vivid in her mind. The way she found him in the backyard, huddled in the rain, his leash coiled around the pole. Around his neck. The guilt had followed her all her life. Like a shadow. Max was her dog, her responsibility. And like a dumb kid, she'd neglected him out there like a common street dog. Papi told her that Max had likely been cold, wanted to break free and get inside. Max must have wound himself around that pole, gotten tangled, and asphyxiated himself. How much he'd suffered, she'd never known.

And here he was, exuberant as ever. She felt the tears pool under her eyes. When she blinked, they cascaded down her cheeks and rolled off her chin. Ramona hugged her dog again and allowed herself to smile. To feel like a little girl again.

"Andres, are you seeing this?" Ramona offered him a glance. Her brother's mouth hung agape as he watched the disfigured man shuffle toward him, his limbs mangled like dead tree branches.

"Hermano!" Andres said.

Once he was close enough, Ramona could see that the man indeed was their brother. Armando's contorted body approached Andres, resting a gentle, gnarled hand on his shoulder.

"Brother," Armando said, his jaw slack, hanging only by the thin strands of leathery skin still attached to it. "I've been waiting here a long time to tell you something."

Andres sobbed.

"I want you to know," Armando said, "that I forgive you."

Andres buried his head in his hands, sniveling like a child.

"I know you didn't mean to run me over. I shouldn't have let you drink that night." Armando turned to Ramona. "I've missed you both."

It was impossible to grasp. But there he was, alive, like Max. Walking, talking miracles. Ramona stood, sprang into Armando's arms, and hugged him, his broken ribs poking against her body. "I missed you so damned much," she said.

Andres wiped the tears from his eyes and joined them in the embrace. She knew guilt had hounded them both, and, like a tick, had nestled itself in the recesses of their minds. Gnawing away at their joy over the years. But for the first time in a long time, things seemed brighter. Like maybe they'd be okay for once.

"Holy shit," Andres said, breaking away as he craned his neck.

Ramona turned and followed his gaze. "Mami," she said under her breath. "Papi." Her heart fluttered. At the entrance of the hedge maze, her mother and father beamed as they waved them over. Armando took Andres's hand, flashed a toothless smile, and began to lead him toward their parents.

Ramona trotted ahead, Max barking excitedly by her side.

Her mother threw her arms wide for a hug, no sign of the stroke that took her two years ago. Ramona recalled every warm moment spent with her; fleeting memories that were never enough to fill the void she'd left. Her father waved her over too, beckoning to her like he did when she was learning to walk. Before the heart attack.

Andres suddenly freed himself from Armando and snatched Ramona's wrist.

"No," Andres said. "Something's wrong."

"What are you talking about?" Ramona said.

"Look at their faces." Andres shook his head. "Look closely."

Ramona studied her parents as they beckoned her. Andres was right. Like abstract paintings, their faces were off, not quite fully realized. They were fuzzy and smoothed over. Devoid of defining features. Like when you held a book in a dream but couldn't quite make out the title or the cover art.

She looked around. Some of the people by the fountain had vanished or had now merged into a single individual or new people altogether. Amalgamations of people she'd known. Friends. Lovers. Acquaintances.

Ramona looked down at Max. His body was now pixelated, blurred to the point he no longer resembled a dog, but the *idea* of a dog. All the things were there: four legs, a muzzle, a tongue, a tail. But his eyes came and went; there one second, and gone the next. He, like the rest, was an unrealized promise, the shadow of a possibility.

This place wasn't real.

She turned to Andres. His face had begun to smooth over. Though it retained its unique shape, his features had begun to bleed into one another. Eyes melding together, nose flattening. She glanced at her hands. They too, now, appeared blurred. This was all a bad dream. A nightmare.

"We're blending into this world," she said. "We have to leave."

"How?" Andres said, his lips shrinking into a thin slit, melding into his face. "Where do we go?"

"The way we came."

Slowly, they backed away from the denizens of Fantastika. The living mirages.

Armando reached out a hand, pleading. "No," he said. "Please stay."

Mami and Papi called out after them. "Stay forever."

Ramona and Andres turned and followed the magenta cobblestone path, scurrying past the garden, past the thicket, over the rolling hills, and through the green pastures. The dream revenants lumbered close behind. Ramona tried to break into a run. As hard as she tried, she couldn't seem to move fast enough. Her legs, for all their pedaling, wouldn't gain enough traction, enough speed. She trudged along like the world had slowed to a crawl.

Armando shambled after them, their parents and Max close behind, his tail slicing the air, distorting it into a spectrum of vibrant, psychedelic colors.

"Stay forever," the nightmares said in unison, their voices a monotonous, flat droning. "Stay forever."

Ramona offered her pursuers another glance. She noticed their feet weren't planted on the ground but were hovering just above the cobblestone path as they ambled closer.

"Please stay."

When they reached the mouth of the cave, Andres took Ramona's hand and squeezed. There was nothing else. Nowhere else to turn. They nodded and lunged into the abyss.

They woke in absolute darkness and drenched in a cold muck. The acrid smell of sulfur was worse now. Ramona felt nauseous, like throwing up. She fumbled blindly on her knees in obscurity, her hands sifting through the thick sludge. Quickly, she turned on her phone's flashlight and waved it around. They were in the bowels of the cellar, its floor covered in the same tar-like substance that had coated the stairs. She helped Andres to his feet. He'd been coated in the slime too.

"What the hell is this?" Andres said trying to shake the gunk off. He removed his jacket and tossed it on the mucky floor. The sweater began to smolder as it dissolved, breaking apart slowly until nothing remained.

"Ouch!" Her fingers began to tingle and burn, like the time she'd touched battery acid. She wiped her hands on her pants and the residue began to perforate the denim.

"Come on," Andres said. "We gotta go. This shit is burning me."

Ramona took a pace forward and kicked something in the dark. She aimed the light at the floor. "Oh my god." A small, partially dissolved mandible protruded from the surface of the tar.

Just then, something stirred. Something wet. She brought her phone toward the source of the sound. She shrieked. The walls. They were pink and fleshy and lined with thousands of squirming follicles, like the cilia that coated the inside of a stomach.

"Holy shit," Andres said. "What is that?"

As if angered by his outburst, the fleshy walls begin to throb and contract. Ramona contemplated the mandible. The gasses. The acidic tar.

Digestive enzymes.

"It's drugged us, made us hallucinate while it tried to digest us," she said. "The cellar is a living thing!"

Andres eyed the cellar doors rattling above as the walls and floor began to spasm and ooze tar. "Or a prison. Come on, let's go!"

Like an inflated sack, the walls bloated outward, the cilia thrashing like hungry feelers. They bolted for the steps. Ramona stumbled over something in the dark, plunging into the tar. Her light caught on a corroded picture frame; the sepia-tinged portrait of a little girl, her face obscured by shattered glass.

Andres helped her to her feet. The walls pressed closer, the cilia lashing at them, catching on their shirts, tearing bits of fabric, and pricking their flesh. They ran up the creaky stairs, the boards protesting under their weight. They came to where the stairs had broken, leaping over the gap. The walls gurgled as the blackness encroached on their backs. Andres shoved the doors open and they dove outside, landing in a tangle of bushes and weeds.

Ramona sprang to her feet and sprinted for the cellar doors. A pair of barbed tendrils penetrated the abyss, lashing at the air around her face. She slammed the doors shut and pressed against them with all her weight. The doors rattled and thumped with a biblical fury. Andres rushed to her side and threw himself against the doors as well. After some time, the pounding ceased and the lurching inside receded until only the sounds of their heavy breaths remained.

A soft, warm breeze fluttered in. A helicopter buzzed overhead and dropped a cascade of water on the dwindling fires in an adjacent field. Plumes of white smoke billowed toward an orange sky as daybreak approached.

Ramona pulled the map from her back pocket and opened her hand, letting the breeze carry it away. Andres wrapped an arm around her shoulder and they started for the car.

For a moment they said nothing to each other. Birds began to chirp somewhere in the distance. The buzz of several helicopters filled the air.

"Was Fantastika real?" Ramona asked, shaking her head. "Or was it in our minds?"

Andres offered the cellar one final glimpse before they rounded the house. He glimpsed the brightening sky. "It was real enough, I guess." When they reached the car, he opened the passenger door and helped her in. "And if it was in our minds, I think our memories were trying to kill us. Maybe it's time we let them go and make new ones."

Ramona nodded.

Andres started the car and drove back down the way they came to look for help.

The Savage Night

Just before the sun set over the horizon, Kushim, the medicine man, heard their dying wails bellow out from beyond the ridge of the ravine. He squeezed the spear in his hand, his feet rolling over a swath of sharp twigs and pebbles as he sprinted toward the terrible cries of his kin.

Kushim winced. He had seen too many winters. His muscles strained and his lungs burned as he sprinted across the valley. He was fortunate to have loyal Akito. His dog ran alongside him, matching his every step.

Suddenly, the screams of men died, and the howls of wolves filled their place. Those fools. He could have helped them fend off those fanged terrors.

For countless seasons he had been their healer, sewing and mending their wounds. And despite this, he had been made to keep his distance from the rest of the tribe, being left to tail them like a bastard child or wounded pack animal.

He scowled as he dwelled on the thought. Not even the warmth of their fires was offered to him any longer.

Jarag, the tribal elder, had accused him of unnatural practices. Rituals that disrupted the harmony between the natural and spirit worlds. His own family had accused him of bringing about bad omens—they feared what they did not understand. But to be an outcast among his own was akin to torture. Regardless, they were all he had in this world.

By the time he and Akito arrived, the sky had turned violet, and the first stars began to shimmer.

The entire tribe was there waiting for him. Men, women, children, even the dogs and their pups. Two dozen bodies lay mangled around the fire, their limbs gnawed and torn from their sockets. Some bellies had been ripped open while their blood and masticated innards spilled out, left to irrigate the ground.

He inspected the wounds. The deep punctures of lupine teeth marked their flesh. Only a large, hungry pack could do this.

Kushim raised his head and lifted his spear to the sky. In wild, twisted tongues he screamed and muttered curses at the gods for their betrayal. They were cries of sadness and anger all at once. He knew not what he said, only that in his heart, he wished his family back.

And so, he pounded his feet in the dirt, dancing the dance of life, hoping that in turn, his spectacle would please the gods and restore existence to the departed.

When his voice became hoarse and he could no longer scream, he ceased the dance. Kushim then set to burying the bodies in a mass grave on the fringes of camp. He laid each member to rest, touching his head to theirs before rolling them into the pit. He capped the site with a mound of stones: one for each person.

As the moon rose, he feasted on the tribe's rations of rabbit giblets, now nearly burned to a crisp as they roasted beside the fire.

He felt a weight press against his chest, and he knew it was loneliness. How would he exist wholly alone now? He turned to Akito and threw him a piece of meat.

Wolves had been stalking the tribe. How could Jarag have been so blind?

As he nestled closer to the fire's warmth, he heard the startling sound of a moan followed by the rustling of dirt.

Akito barked. Kushim spun around, his spear cocked. The sound of shifting soil came again, only louder this time. The noise arose from the direction of the grave.

It couldn't be.

Kushim stepped forward, his eyes narrowing as he focused on the darkness ahead. Another moan. Akito's lips curled as he snarled in response.

"Aughh. Aughhhh," a familiar voice groaned.

A bloodied arm sprang from the earth, its hand clawing at the air. Kushim dropped the spear and clutched the arm. He heaved with all his strength until, like a root, he plucked a man out from the grave.

Dragul writhed and convulsed in agony atop the bloodied soil, his trunk missing both right arm and leg, while a deep gash ran like a fissure atop his head. As Dragul opened his mouth to groan, Kushim peered inside. His tongue had been ripped apart; blood seeped from his maw like crushed berries.

70

Kushim nuzzled his head to Dragul's and carried him toward the fire's warmth. There in the light, he gauged Dragul's injuries.

The man's body was severely maimed. The work of wolves. He was certain now, as their saliva still bubbled on the man's punctured flesh.

Dragul reached his hand out to Kushim, pleading for an end to it all. Kushim clenched his teeth in response. How could Kushim end this man's life? He'd be left to face the horrors of the world, alone, without a companion.

Akito approached Dragul and licked the blood from the open wound where his shoulder bone lay exposed. Kushim flailed his arms and shooed the dog away.

Kushim pulled madly on his hair, groaning as he struggled to think of a solution. Then, he smiled. If he hurried, there was a chance it could work. He sprinted for the burial mound and retrieved the body of another man, Kalkama, whose throat had been pierced and crushed by the same lupine teeth. Kushim examined his body. Besides a few scrapes, his limbs were intact. He dragged Kalkama and set his corpse beside Dragul, whose skin had turned pale from the loss of blood.

Kushim retrieved his stone knife and thrust it into Kalkama's right shoulder. He made an incision into the meat and cut until the arm was severed.

He did the same with his right leg, grumbling as he sawed deep into the bone.

Kushim uttered a prayer under his breath and proceeded to insert Kalkama's arm and leg into the missing gaps in Dragul's body. He entwined the sinew and ligaments to the bone and muscle until they were a part of Dragul. He then sealed Dragul's wounds by thrusting his knife into the fire, removing it, and pressing the heated stone blade to his skin.

Dragul screamed until he nearly passed into darkness.

Kushim retrieved a deer stomach pouch and tilted it to Dragul's lips, wherein he gently poured some water inside his mouth.

After a while, Dragul fell into sleep.

Kushim mumbled soft, rapid words directed at the gods. His prayer was the only magic he could invoke. It would have to do.

Kushim would fight for Dragul's life lest he displease the gods and the spirits of the tribe. Lest he be alone in this world. Amidst the distant howls of wolves, Kushim cradled Dragul's cold body until the sun rose.

Ten moons and ten suns had passed. For all of Kushim's mending chants and remedies,

Dragul remained dumb, and his right limbs partially paralyzed. All the hair had fallen from his scalp, and his skin remained pale like death. To Kushim's dismay, his companion could not throw a spear as before.

Hunting had become difficult for them during the day as the animals became frightened of his uncontrollable shrieks. With his frail body and the knowledge that most predators hunted during the day, Dragul afforded Kushim little choice. The men adopted the nighttime as their domain.

On this night, while they approached their next meal, Kushim placed a hand on Dragul's chest and motioned for him to remain silent. Akito stalked noiselessly through the weeds, moving alongside his master. Kushim stepped forward, both hands clutching his spear should anything spring forth from the darkness. Nothing stirred except the soft buzzing of the mosquitoes as they wisped past his head.

There, splayed out on the grass lay their dinner. It had almost been picked apart completely, but Kushim whispered a prayer to the spirit of the animal nevertheless. The corpse was a gift that would not go to waste.

Tonight, they would feast on the carrion remains of a mountain goat. Kushim knelt beside its open ribcage, scraping apart the hanging shreds of meat from its fur with his knife. He tossed a handful of raw flesh to Dragul, who immediately set about devouring his meal. He bit into the meat like a crazed beast, pulling on the flesh until it snapped apart, strand by strand. The blood that coated his face lay in stark contrast to the pale moonlight that now tinted his body. Dragul had become bestial. Half alive, half dead. Like a reflection in a pond, it was similar to a man but not real.

Lowering a ribbon of meat into his own mouth, Kushim noticed the two large, deep puncture marks embedded in the neck of the goat. A long-fanged cat must have roamed these lands in the daytime. It would be best to return to the cave before it came back.

Kushim looked to the sky. The sun would rise soon, and the terrors of the world would come to claim the land once more.

After their meal, the three of them departed for the cavern alongside the coast, where the waves crashed against the rocks like thunder.

They entered the cave, greeted by the throng of bats hanging on the ceiling of the cavern. They screeched and fluttered like restless birds. Dragul took curiosity in their fervor, mimicking their cries, before losing interest and curling into his own body as sleep took him.

The sun rose on the horizon, and Kushim felt the weight surface in his chest once more. The pain traveled with him despite Dragul's company. He embraced Akito and wondered why the gods had not gifted him with another family and instead cursed him with a ravenous shell of a man who could not think, speak, or hunt.

Then as the tears rolled down his face, sleep took him, too.

Dragul groaned as the last of the water trickled down his cracked lips. The pouch had nothing else to offer, and there had been no source of water as far as Kushim could see. The back of his throat felt dry and coarse now, burning with every breath.

They sat quietly on a small hill overlooking the plain. No animals stirred or cried out, not even the smell of rotting flesh permeated the air around them. The wolves were silent, and the tracks of the long-fanged cats were nowhere to be found.

Beyond the plains, the woods rolled as far as Kushim could see, but that trek would take them another night's travel.

Kushim grunted and cursed the gods for abandoning them and leaving them to starve and thirst.

As the moonlight glimmered on his body, Dragul rolled in the dirt, flailing his arms like a child. Kushim knelt beside him, placing a hand on his mouth to silence his cries, but the man bit into his palm. Kushim yelled and jerked his hand free. A small piece of flesh had torn loose, spilling blood down his wrist. Dragul licked his lips and reached his hands out to Kushim.

Kushim lightly jabbed his spear into Dragul's midsection. Dragul's legs buckled, sending him stumbling to the ground.

Kushim dwelled on his hand before returning his gaze to the man on the ground. Dragul brought both hands to his mouth and motioned to his lips, screeching like a cave bat.

Kushim retrieved his knife and cut deep into his palm until the blood flowed freely. He raised his arm and let the blood trickle into Dragul's mouth.

Dragul knelt underneath the stream with his mouth agape. The blood poured into his maw, and the pale man drank until the flow stopped. He then crawled toward a bloody puddle that had collected on the floor and lapped it up like a dog.

The night began to give way to the morning, and Dragul turned to Kushim, baring his teeth, his gums stained red. He was smiling.

Kushim turned away and tried to push the image from his mind for fear that his dreams would match the horrors of reality.

The burning pain boring deep into his neck woke him. Then came the warmth of liquid flowing down his skin. He opened his eyes in the dark of the cave, Dragul's red face greeting him, his teeth latched firmly onto his throat. Over their heads, the bats thrashed their wings and shrieked wildly.

Kushim thrust his right hand into his pouch, retrieved his knife, and plunged it into Dragul's left shoulder. Dragul's grip on his throat loosened while he howled in pain. Kushim shoved Dragul from his body and turned to reach for his spear but found it already embedded in Akito's carcass. The dog's body had been split down the middle, half of his innards missing.

Before he could turn back to Dragul, the man-beast leaped onto Kushim, knocking him to the floor. Dragul wrapped two icy hands around Kushim's neck. He opened his mouth, bearing forth his rotting teeth. His breath carried the rancid promise of death and decay. Kushim lifted a knee and bucked him over his head.

Dragul landed on his skull, and the sound of crunching bones echoed through the cave. Kushim pushed himself off the floor and hobbled toward the cavern entrance. Dragul's wounded howls echoed shrilly across the mouth of the cave.

Kushim thought of turning to face Dragul one last time but decided against it and limped away.

Kushim heard Dragul's wails fade over time as he trekked toward the rolling plains.

He placed a hand over his throat, meandering through the wild, tripping over fallen branches. The night was cold and unforgiving, the breeze nipping at his skin as he struggled to move his legs.

Until by chance, under the light of the moon, he stumbled into another tribe's camp. Startled and woken by his grunts, the strange people looked upon him in confusion while he fell to his knees. He extended two pleading hands while the blood poured from the wounds on his neck.

He tried to speak, but the words would not form. Only the wet, guttural sounds of a dying man escaped his lips. He knew then that he would not be able to warn them of the abomination who had been resurrected from death only to be sewn anew from the body of another; who traveled by night and shrieked like a bat; who drank the blood of men and beasts alike.

And before the world faded to darkness, he mustered the last words he would speak and prayed the warning would suffice.

"Dragul," he said as his last breath left his body.

Then under the gaze of strangers, the night took him for all time.

The Bottom Dweller

1.

It was ten minutes to midnight when Jasper Marvins shuffled inside The Mess Hall, stretching and yawning. He expected the usual ruckus typical of late-shift park ambassadors milling around shooting the shit, complaining of the long haul to come. Instead, the dining room was silent. A handful of employees sat staring at the walls, tapping their fingers on the tables. The puffy bags under their eyes and dead-fish-like slackened jaws spoke of many sleepless nights. He felt their pain.

The Mess Hall wasn't usually open to park employees. This restaurant, located deep in the belly of the *Pequod*, The Realm of the Deep's enormous "submarine," was reserved for guests during open hours. But during the late shift, Jasper and his fellow workers got to dine on crab cakes and cod fillets beneath a cornucopia of lobster buoys, nautical knots, and Victorian sailors' portraits. Squinting sidelong through a porthole, Jasper caught a glimpse of animated squid hurtling upward from some deeper hunting ground.

He set his tray beside an old man hunched over a steaming bowl of chowder. His stomach rumbled as he broke off the tail of a crawfish and dangled its bright flesh in front of his mouth. Peculiar blue swirls patterned the meat, like galaxies in miniature. Frowning, Jasper peered closer, the design mesmerizing him with its speckled, spiraling arms. If he didn't know better, he could've almost sworn they were spinning. He shook his head. Couldn't be. Just markings, just camouflage. Some peculiar bioluminescent phenotype evolved in the lightless depths.

He dropped the crawfish tail back onto his plate. His hunger had suddenly faded. He rubbed his eyes and took a sip of coffee, hoping it might clear the cobwebs from his mind. He just needed to wake up; that was it. He was seeing things. He was lucky to have the job, graveyard shift or not; and now wasn't the time to risk a psych evaluation by ranting about luminescent sea creatures. This Realm was already plenty weird as it was.

"What's the matter, boy," asked a drawling voice to his left. "You don't like mudbugs?"

"Huh?" Jasper glanced up.

"Mudbugs." The man's face was a wreckage of scars and two-day-old beard. "Crawfish? Bottom feeders? Name's Tyler, by the way." He put out a thick-fingered hand.

"Got it," Jasper said, forcing a smile. "Sorry, not from around here, Tyler. I like 'em alright, just not that hungry, I guess." He dwelled again on the strange spirals marking the crustacean's tail. "Never seen crawfish this fancy," he said prodding the tail with his fork. "Are these local?"

Tyler shrugged. "Fresh, free seafood, that's all I know. One of the many perks of working in The Deep. Eat up, boy! Big day tomorrow. They gonna work you hard tonight."

"Yeah," Jasper said, sliding his dish away. "Summer season starts tomorrow, I know. Looks like quittin' time for you, though."

"Yep." Tyler eased back into his chair. "Earned it, too. Been a hell of a day. Working out some kinks on Mariana Trench Dive. Sometimes the submersible gets caught on the tracks right when the Hive Queen pops out."

Jasper's eyes widened. "You're a technosopher?"

Tyler shrugged. "Ride engineer. 'Round here, we call it the Mayhem Prevention Department. Fixing stalled rides is the least of it. Can you imagine explaining to Dalton why a busload of first-graders are stuck on a submarine, beggin' to be let off?"

"I wouldn't want to be in that meeting," Jasper agreed.

Tyler huffed. "Me neither. You got kids?"

Jasper shook his head and frowned. "No. Maybe I'm a nihilist, or maybe I'm afraid, but I can't really see myself bringing any into this world, the way things are right now. It would be far too cruel an act. Besides, I couldn't handle that kind of pressure."

"I hear that," Tyler raised his coffee cup in toast.

"What was that thing you said?" Jasper asked. "The Hive Queen?"

"That's what we call her," Tyler sipped his coffee. "Rumor has it she's Teague's fever dream of a sea creature he once encountered in a Mexican cenote. Just a Texas tall tale, though, I reckon. You ask me, she's one of Egger's monsters."

Jasper tilted his head. "Lot of legends around Dalton Teague."

"To say the least," Tyler agreed, chuckling. "Some say he's more than just human—though I'm skeptical of such claims, myself. Hey, what'd they bring you on for, anyway?"

"Me? I'm just a tank cleaner." Jasper suddenly remembered his own coffee. He stirred in cream and sugar as he gave the short version of his story. "I was a diver in the Navy. Did a tour in 'Nam, so I guess that impressed them enough to give me a shot. Tonight's my first shift."

"Hm." Tyler's smile faded and he stirred his chowder. "Big tanks. Lots of fishies. I heard Teague has a lot of pets in there. Personal collection, some say."

"Um," Jasper gulped. "What happened to the last cleaner? Did he get fired?"

Tyler suddenly broke into a fit of coughing, eyes flicking wildly to the right.

Startled, Jasper looked up to see a tall, slender man in a gray three-piece suit and a pale complexion standing beside them, arms folded behind his back.

"Good evening, Mr. Marvins." The man adjusted his thick-lensed glasses, just as he had in Jasper's job interview. *What was his name?* Right: Kurtz; Byron Kurtz, overnight marine-life supervisor. A disturbing smile now stretched across his face. "Would you be so kind as to follow me?" Kurtz extended an arm, making it clear this invitation wasn't optional.

Jasper nodded a goodbye to Tyler, taking a final gulp of coffee before dumping his food in the trash and following Kurtz out of The Mess Hall. His stomach twisted in knots, and he wasn't sure it was from hunger.

2.

It was a long, silent walk to the locker room, where Kurtz asked Jasper to change into his wetsuit. By the time Jasper had squirmed into the rubbery contraption, Kurtz was waiting for him at the door, hands folded behind his back. He wore no expression other than a mild smile that didn't reach his eyes.

"Mr. Marvins," he said. "Thank you so much for being a part of our crew here in the Realm of the Deep."

"I should be thanking you, sir." Jasper gulped again, wondering where this was all going.

"Here at OmniPark, we all consider one another family. Some even like to think of Dalton himself as our loving grandfather. At any rate, family looks out for one another—wouldn't you agree?" Kurtz swept a hand toward the hallway, beckoning Jasper onward. All he could do was follow.

They wove through a maze of lamp-lit backrooms and brass-knobbed corridors, finally reaching an antique pull-cord elevator that transported them to a level Jasper hadn't visited yet.

The doors accordioned open, revealing a staging area the size of an aircraft hangar. A series of rafters and catwalks zig-zagged along the ceiling, coalescing into a platform that jutted out over a pool of water stretching the length of a football field. A dozen, clammy-skinned men in wetsuits leaned on the support rails, watching him with the same sleepless look as the employees in The Mess Hall. Each of them carried an aluminum pail in one hand and a spade in the other.

Jasper waved in greeting. The men stood motionless, unsmiling, eyes unblinking.

"Our filters aren't working properly," Kurtz explained. "We've been experiencing a buildup of debris. Food particles, we believe. You're going to need to inspect the filter, which you'll find about thirty feet down, on the left-hand side of the tank. Let's get you into the right gear."

Kurtz waved at the men above. They slowly lowered a winch grasping a bulky atmospheric diving suit. The suit reminded Jasper of Robby the Robot with its mix of concentric spheres, ball and socket joints, and exaggerated bubble helmet. He ran a hand over the gear. A fusion of thick plastic, rubber, and metal components lined the suit like some space-age armor.

Jasper glanced at the men on the rafters again. "Who are they?" he said nodding his head in their direction. "What are the buckets for?"

Kurtz adjusted his glasses, wiping off a smudge with the handkerchief in his pocket. "Those are our cleaners. We use the pails to collect some of the—ah...larger waste, which our filters are unable to dispense of."

Jasper scanned the staging area. A set of flickering fluorescent lights hung from the ceiling, casting a pale glow over the tranquil waters below. He stepped toward the pool and felt a wave of heat wash over him.

He turned to Jasper. "A little hot for a saltwater tank, isn't it?"

Kurtz placed a hand on Jasper's shoulder and gazed down into the pool, a grin spreading across his tight-skinned face. "We have quite a few tanks in the Realm of the Deep, each housing different species of marine animals. We've compartmentalized different sections in order to simulate their different environments. This tank in particular," he said pointing directly below, "provides a home for a number of...

unique bottom-dwelling organisms, whose natural habitat is near hydrothermal vents. We keep the temperature just below boiling, though we often have trouble calibrating the thermostat. Which is the reason for the heavy dive suit you'll be donning."

"Bottom-dwelling organisms," Jasper repeated. "Like the Hive Queen?"

"The Hive Queen," Kurtz said, wiping a bead of sweat from his brow, "is only a toy to frighten children. You should know that by now. No, this…" He shook his head. "This is something entirely different, I'm afraid."

Jasper peered down into the pool. His reflection stared back. Glimmering blue spirals unspooled in the blackness of his pupils. He turned away, shivering despite the heat and prepared to submerge.

3.

After a crew of engineers fit him into the diving suit, the men in the rafters docked a tether into its spine and submerged him into the murky waters. Immersed in the boiling green brine, he felt like he was cooking alive, even within the protective gear.

As he descended, he noticed a glass barrier on his right-hand side separating his tank from another. Finding his balance in weightlessness, he scanned the adjoining tank, astonished at the variety of aquatic life gliding effortlessly about.

A manta ray barrel rolled gracefully alongside the barrier, its skin glistening under the bright lights. A multitude of bright-colored fish zipped past, then assembled into a large body, and finally banked away as a cohesive unit.

Jasper broke his gaze from the fish and realized the tether had plunged him farther down. He'd been so entranced he'd somehow lost track of time and distance. He shook his head. *Focus*. Here, the waters began to cloud with small particles and the light from above started to fade. He looked up. The distorted outlines of the men on the rafters were barely visible as they peered down on him. His hand probed the top of his bubble helmet for the lamp switch. He found it, flicked it on, and a sharp beam of light cut across the dark water.

The tank's floor was now in view. It had been designed like a rocky, jagged trench and housed barnacles, long, snaking tube worms, and a plethora of zoarcid fish and gastropods. He swung his arms and drifted toward the left side of the tank, where three hoses curved out from the stony floor and fed into a large pump six-feet long. As he checked the fitting for any signs of leakage, he noted the abysmal water quality, caused by food particles, feces, and sediment.

Something glimmered in his peripheral vision just below his feet. About two yards down, nestled in a depression in the rocks, a mound of fleshy, translucent spheres shimmered like stars. Jasper allowed himself to drop down to the bottom of the tank. Once he balanced his feet on the rocks, he focused his light on the spheres. The light penetrated their thin membranes, revealing little squirming embryos inside.

Jasper scanned a network of artificial coral that ran along the leftmost wall of the tank, trying to spot what could have laid the eggs. A small octopus darted past his leg and disappeared into the rocks, raising a storm of sediment across the water. He gave up his search and traced a fingertip along the thin outer membrane of one of the eggs. The walls had a fleshy, gelatinous consistency, coated with a slimy algae-like residue. He pressed gently against the surface, which bent inward without breaking.

Suddenly, a thousand tiny hooks lashed out at his back, tearing through the tether and the protective metal of the suit, ripping into his skin. The barbs tugged at him, spinning him forcefully around. A spindly leg slashed at his helmet, cracking it. A current of boiling-hot water began to seep through the crack, hissing and steaming in the minuscule space between his face and the lens.

Through the steam, Jasper's lamplight illuminated his attacker. He gazed into a pair of round, obsidian eyes. Like some twisted crustacean, a thick, serrated carapace guarded its head while rows upon rows of legs clawed up and down its belly until its body tapered off into a long, curved tail. The crustacean dwarfed him by about six feet, even now in its semi-curled state.

Jasper screamed into his helmet, the blistering water now rushing into his mouth, scalding his tongue. The beast sank another dozen scythe-like swimmerets into his suit, hooking his belly, pulling him closer. Spindly flagella shot outward from its underbelly, sending hot pain lancing outward from his groin. His abdominal muscles throbbed and burned as a thousand red-hot needles threaded through his body. He swung his legs upwards, bringing his knees close to his chest. He planted his feet on the creature's belly and tried to push off, but his strength had already faded. His limbs went limp, and he felt himself dragged toward the creature like a helpless doll.

The monstrosity whipped its antennae through his helmet, his temples, digging them deep behind his eyes.

A barrage of images flashed his mind's eye like distorted television channels: spiraling galaxies scattered across the void; colorful planets whirling around alien suns; crustaceans mating with otherworldly lifeforms; a planet resembling earth; a vessel plunging into the depths of a cenote; complete submersion in a dark, frigid lake; the warm, waking waters of a new home; the stern smile of Dalton Teague; eggs hatching; a pack of men scooping her children away; his own, thrashing body impaled on countless rows of legs.

His thoughts centered back on The Mess Hall and the markings embedded on the flesh of his dinner. He heard Tyler's voice echo in his mind: *"Fresh, free seafood... one of the many perks you get working here."* A flood of nausea washed over him as he fought the urge to regurgitate.

Jasper didn't know how, but every image suddenly made sense. History made real through their bond. And the blue swirls: star maps embedded into their being, a genetic language encoding the history of a race of spacefarers seeking to integrate biodiversity into their essence. Every spiral, a visited galaxy. Star to star, planet to planet, the seeds of every compatible lifeform were propagated through their eggs.

The antennae withdrew from his brain and the assault of imagery ceased. Then, the pain returned to his body.

His helmet had now flooded with the boiling, briny water. Through his burning eyes he watched as the creature dispersed a cloudy white mist into the fleshy mound beneath them. Jasper's heart beat like a piston. He wanted to cry. Maybe he already was.

The eggs began to throb, pulsing in time like a clutch of hearts. One by one, they popped, releasing tiny creatures scurrying along the aquarium floor.

The creature opened its mandibles, and Jasper gazed upward one last time, toward a surface he would never see again. Far above him—much too far for him to see or hear—the men on the rafters raised their spades and pails, banging them together in celebration. Kurtz's silhouette stood motionless, his hands at his back. Jasper thought he saw a smile crack across his distorted face.

The creature's mandible pulled Jasper's head gently into its maw.

Your worst fear has come true, it spoke into his mind. *You are to be a father. Thank you, my mate, for the gift of your life.*

Its mandibles snapped, and darkness flooded in.

Adrift Ebon Tides

Like a lily pad drifting helplessly down a river's currents, soft waves rocked the life raft deeper into sea. Leandro turned to look behind himself until the light of the flames engulfing the ship finally vanished behind the dark horizon, leaving only a dome of glittering stars above. He looked back at Paul Mahoney, who had now taken to wrapping his arms around his chest.

Leandro stuck a thumb in his mouth and chewed on his nail. "I had no choice. You saw it too, right? Whatever that was?"

Mahoney looked down at his neoprene boots and nodded. The young fisherman looked like a corpse in the darkness, his lips purple, his face blue.

"Maybe some of the guys are still alive," Leandro said.

"Maybe," Mahoney said softly. "I hope not."

Leandro nodded and leaned over the side of the raft. The moon's pallid reflection was round and bright upon the surface of the ocean, breaking its endless ebon monotony. He inhaled a whiff of briny air and wished so desperately to be back ashore, holding his grandson on the docks as the waves crashed against the rocks.

What he'd witnessed tonight had no place in this world. Any world. He'd burn the whole planet down if it meant never having to see that thing again. Then, he thought about the rest of the crew.

His heart started to burn a hole through his chest. He tried to push the guilt back down into his belly and told himself he did what had to be done. Though the more he dwelt on it, the less sure he was of what exactly had happened. Everything transpired so quickly, his mind was struggling to grasp what he'd seen. Impossible things. Horrible things. Things that made him want to gouge his eyes out.

Yes, it had to be done. There was no other way.

The surface of the water broke and the moon's reflection began to phase in and out of existence. He leaned back inside the raft and watched as a swell of sargassum swarmed the dinghy like flies over a carcass. A shudder ran up his spine at the sight of the tangled mass of seaweed, piling higher and higher around the raft, like long, wet strands of hair.

Leandro's teeth gnashed against his thumb until it had numbed completely. "We won't last long like this. Any idea where we are?"

Mahoney shook his head.

"Me neither." Leandro sighed. The skin on his arms erupted with goosebumps as the frigid air nipped at his body. "Any family back home?"

"Two kids," Mahoney said.

"Great. What are their names?"

The man in front of him bit his lip and remained silent for a long moment. He began to rock back and forth, clutching his shoulders as if something was going to whisk him away into the night. Perhaps he wasn't wrong. "I can't remember."

"You can't remember?"

"No," he said, looking around. "Why are we here?"

Leandro opened his mouth to speak but stopped himself. He plumbed the depths of his mind, sifting for a piece of something that was now missing. He looked up at the man who was now a stranger. "I don't know."

Something moved in his peripheral vision. An unexplainable blur. A flash of light. He looked up at the sky. The stars were now bending in peculiar ways, their light twisting into impossible ribbons. He turned to his companion, curious if he'd been seeing the same thing, but the man's head had been smoldering, his pink flesh partially melted. Small things wriggled in the dark of his eye sockets. Leandro leaned forward, hoping to make out what it was. He fought the urge to vomit when the maggots spilled out onto the floor of the raft.

Leandro rubbed his eyes with his palms. When he opened them again, the man's face had been restored, but his own hands were now coated with blood, the warm, viscous fluid pooling at his boots. His thumb had been gnawed off, leaving a large chunk of exposed bone. He spat out a wad of blood and cursed under his breath. What the hell was going on? If it was a dream, he wanted nothing more than to wake.

He eyed his masticated thumb again. He was lucky the cold had numbed the pain. Not knowing what to do, he tucked his bleeding hand into his armpit and clenched his teeth. In this cold it was only a matter of time before his organs shut down. Soon, they'd both die of exposure.

For what seemed a lifetime neither man said anything, each nestled in his corner of the raft as wisps of vapor crept out their mouths and faded into the night sky. "I'm cold," his raftmate finally said.

"Me too," Leandro said.

Leandro's raftmate pursed his lips and reached into a compartment by his side. He slung an emergency kit at his feet and sorted through its contents. Gauze, bandages, mylar blankets. Shrugging, he tossed them into the ocean.

"No point," his raftmate said.

Leandro nodded.

His raftmate's hand trembled as he retrieved a flare gun from the kit. He ogled it in wonder for a moment, turning it this way and that in his grasp. When he'd spent enough time looking over the thing, he stuck the barrel in his mouth and pulled the trigger. There came a resounding pop and a geyser of blood spewed out the back of his head. In the darkness, the man's maw flickered like a jack-o'-lantern, the fire crackling like a scrambled television channel. The man's limbs dropped limply at his sides and in moments his head was completely ablaze.

Leandro sat there and gazed at the beauty of it all. The way the flaming tendrils lapped up the man's head like a torch, the way the fire's aura lit the endless black ocean. The heat felt immaculate on his face. Leandro shuffled across the raft and embraced the man and his gracious heat. The flames began to spread over his clothes, his flesh, even catching on his beard like tinder. Before the fire enveloped him, he offered the sky one last glimpse. The stars ceased their twinkling, their light now suspended in animation as they watched him like unblinking eyes. It was the last moment he ever knew fear. For that, he was thankful.

Midnight Shoeshine

Archie LaRue's shoes tapped against the floorboards, shattering the silence of an empty boardwalk on Christmas night. The vendors had long shuttered their doors, most of them, permanently. It was just as well. People could seldom afford to partake in leisurely strolls along the beach these days. Times were different now. He didn't blame them. Not one bit.

He exhaled a deep sigh while he strolled past an empty carousel and the nearby sounds of a Wurlitzer chiming its cheerful tunes. It had been far too long since he'd last brought Camille and Bobby, the result of a demanding acting career which, recently, had gone bust. Now, he'd never get the chance to bring them again. Not after Camille ran off the way she did.

He turned toward the Santa Monica pier and dipped his head as a frigid breeze swept against his body, nipping at his hands like small razors. The wind blew a newspaper across the floor until it wrapped its pages around his leg. He plucked it and held it against the light from a lamppost. It was an October issue of the *Los Angeles Times*. The day the markets crashed. He scoffed and released the paper, offering it back to the wind.

Ahead, a string of lampposts flickered and buzzed erratically, casting eerie, dancing shadows upon the planks of the old pier. If he hadn't been drunk, he would've sworn on his mother's grave that he saw the shadows of three shapes scuttling underneath the floorboards. He mumbled a prayer under his breath and made his way to the tip of the dock where the waves crashed against the pillars below.

Archie leaned forward and scanned the ocean. Nothing but darkness waiting to swallow him whole. It was just as well. He'd exit the stage on his terms, for once. He planted a foot over the bottom rail and hoisted himself onto the ledge. His insides twisted themselves into knots, his body offering protest to his final intended act.

"Hey, Mister," he heard a soft voice cry out.

Archie turned to find a young, disheveled boy, no older than ten, stepping forth from the shadows. His face had been smudged with grease and his clothes looked like they hadn't been washed in weeks, perhaps months. The boy nestled a shoeshine box under one arm and wrapped the other around his chest. His purple lips quivered before opening them to speak. "Care for a shoeshine?"

"Christ Almighty, boy," Archie said, startled, "you're gonna die out in this cold." He scanned the pier for a sign of the boy's parents. Nothing, not even a single drunkard stumbling across the boardwalk. "What are you doing in the middle of the night offering shoeshines?"

"Things have been rough," he said, scratching his cheek, smearing the grease on his face. "My pop just up and left after he lost his job. I'm just trying to feed my family."

Archie nodded. "Admirable. What's your name?"

"Eloy, sir. Nice to meet you. So whaddaya say?"

"Kid," Archie said, pursing his lips. He considered telling Eloy what he was about to do. Thought about telling the kid to turn and walk away as he took the plunge into the void. Then, he thought better of it and shrugged. "Eloy. What makes you think I need a shoeshine?"

"You've got a beautiful pair on your feet," he said, nodding at Archie's shoes. "But in their current state, how's anyone supposed to appreciate them?"

His two-toned wingtips had dulled and caked with booze and mud, vestiges of countless nights ambling drunk about town. "What's it matter to anyone what my shoes look like?"

Eloy smiled. "A man's gotta look good no matter where he's going. Besides, I promise you'll feel better the minute I'm done."

Archie regarded Eloy for a moment. A clean haircut, a good shower and the kid wouldn't look too different from Bobby. He bit his lip and fought the urge to cry. "Alright, kid, you got yourself a customer." He hopped off the rail and patted Eloy's shoulder.

"Thanks, Mister. My family will be eternally grateful." Eloy knelt and unpacked his rags, his eyes gleaming with joy. Archie placed a foot on his rickety box and crossed both arms over his chest, the night progressively getting colder as his body burned through the liquor.

"You smell like my pop," Eloy said as he got to work.

"How's that?"

"Gin and Tonic. It was his favorite. He said whenever he was having a bad day, a little went a long way."

"What's your point?"

"You must be having a bad day. You can tell me about it. Everyone should let off a little steam."

"Kid," he said, shaking his head, "not that it matters to you, but I've lost everything."

"Lot of people losing their jobs, lately."

Eloy ran a cloth across his shoe, scrubbing off the filth the last two months had brought him. His tiny fingers were white from the cold, but his face showed no signs of discomfort. Archie supposed he was just happy to land a client at this time.

"No, I don't just mean my job. I lost my savings, my investments. My wife left and took my son Bobby with her. Said I'm no good to them without money. How's that for family support?"

"I'm sorry, Mister. What did you used to do?"

"You ever been to a moving picture show?"

Eloy shook his head, ashamed. "I don't get out much during the day." He retrieved a vial of shoe polish and applied it generously across the crusted leather.

"It's alright. It's a dead art, anyway. They're making those new sound pictures. Lots of old actors losing their jobs on account they can't remember so many lines of dialogue."

Eloy smiled and nodded, keeping his eyes focused on his task. He dismissed Archie's first shoe and brought up his other, settling it gently on the box. He rummaged through his tools, sifting aside a hammer, assorted nails, and a filthy sponge, until he found a fresh rag. He then set to scrubbing the shoe.

The wind blew fiercely as it tugged on Archie's sweater vest. A shiver ran along his limbs, turning his hairs prickly. Now, more than anything, he wanted to disregard the whole idea. He wanted to nestle his tired body in his warm bed and forget the whole thing. He sniffled and regarded Eloy, unflinching as he toiled away. He wondered if he'd doomed Bobby to a similar fate. No. He shook at the thought. There was still time to make things right. There had to be.

"All done," Eloy said, tossing his rags back into the box.

Archie's shoes glistened in the flickering light of the pier. They looked the way they used to when he was on top, when he used to be someone. He gazed at the poor boy. The wind blew tufts of his hair over his pale face. He was malnourished and scraping by in dangerous places no child should ever be in. "Hey, Eloy," Archie said, digging for change in his pockets. "Where's your family live?"

His cheeks flushed. "We don't have a home."

"Listen, I've got a nice, big house not too far from here." Archie bent over and placed a half-dollar coin in Eloy's box. "How would you and your family like to—"

Eloy snatched the hammer and brought it down against the back of Archie's head. All Archie heard was the wet crunch before the sound of the waves became muted. His skull throbbed and his legs buckled, sending his body collapsing onto the cold, wet planks. Eloy lunged at him and sank his teeth into his throat. Archie opened his mouth to scream but could only produce a wisp of vapor. The warmth of blood cascading down his neck brought small relief against the night's chill.

The flickering lights illuminated the twisted forms of a woman and a young girl crawling forth from the underbelly of the pier. They approached, snarling like rabid dogs, sets of fangs protruding from their mouths. Their faces were as gaunt and pale and hungry as the boy's. Archie stretched out a hand and tried to pull himself forward, but all strength had left his body. He thought once more of Camille and Bobby. He allowed himself to dwell on only the happy moments. Then, Eloy and the terrors knelt beside him, each plunging their teeth into his flesh, until the darkness greeted him forever.

The Last Train out of Calico

The train's headlight cut through the night like a phantom flame. If there had been a voice of hesitation in Felix Hidalgo's head, it was drowned out by the thundering roar of the cranks and wheels rolling across the mountain pass.

It was just as well. There could be no room for doubt. Not now that they had grown frail, their reflexes dulled by time.

"It will be here soon," Luis Villareal said. He adjusted his eyepatch and loaded his revolver with a slow, shaky hand, his one good eye struggling to account for depth. Satisfied, he snapped the cylinder shut and scowled.

"I wonder if our bodies are still up for it," Nails Benson said, pulling his duster tight as a gust blew in. "Ain't done this in a long time, fellas. My bones are achin'."

Irving Thompson fastened his wrinkled Union Army kepi over his balding head. It was a relic from his glory days long ago. "If the spirit is willing," he said, "there is nothing a man can't do."

Warren Blackhawk sat quietly atop his horse like a statue. The veteran Lakota warrior's sagging eyes squinted as light flickered through the windows of the passenger cars like fireflies.

Jake Emery tied a red bandana over his face and followed Blackhawk's gaze. "If we mess this up," he said, his voice gruff, "we'll be strung from the gallows and buried at Boot Hill cemetery like the other banditos."

Hidalgo licked his cracked lips and patted the side of his horse's neck, more for his own reassurance than the horse's. "No point talking like that," he said. "We will pull this off. And if we don't, it won't matter because we will be dead long before the gallows, amigos."

"The Jefe's right," Thompson said. "Besides, what awaits us on that train will be enough to have us living comfortably 'til the end of our days. That is worth the risk in my estimation."

Emery shook his head. "How can we be sure? Don't none of us know what's in there."

The train plowed west through the darkness, curving along the base of the Calico Mountains. A jet of steam billowed into the wide, obsidian sky, briefly veiling a small swath of stars.

Benson folded his arms over his chest. "All that talk about the miners finding something inside that mountain means whatever's in there's gotta be big. Why else ship their cargo off on the last train out of Calico in such a hurry?"

"And under the cover of night, no less," Thompson said. "They must have hit a silver vein. They're sending some off to Los Angeles to procure more supplies."

Emery nodded.

The train blasted its horn, sending birds darting from the Joshua trees like scattershot.

"It is time," Hidalgo said.

Villareal reached into his saddlebag and dispersed five sticks of dynamite; one for each other man. He slid his own stick into his bandolier. "This will scare them good, no?" he said smirking as he twirled his gray whiskers.

Under the moonlight, the men looked worn and gaunt, like pale blue corpses. They'd shed their youth like a snake sheds its skin. Yet, in spirit, they remained the same bastards he'd always known them to be. Hearts of steel and fire. Hidalgo knew he wouldn't do this with anyone else.

"Expect some hired guns on that train," Thompson said, pulling his old cavalry gloves over his hands. He carefully unsheathed his old saber and gave it a lookover before sliding it back into the scabbard. "Do not hesitate to shoot every last living man if it comes to it. Just like the old days."

"Amigo," Hidalgo turned to the young, red-haired kid he'd picked up at the saloon earlier that day. The young man, not older than eighteen, shivered atop his horse, a lasso spooled around his right shoulder. "You know the plan. We will stop the train down the track. You will meet us with the horses, and we'll split our earnings with you. Entendido? Understand?"

The kid nodded. "Y-yes, sir."

Hidalgo smiled. "Muy bien, muchacho." He faced the rest of the men and tipped his hat.

The men whooped and hollered, bolting headlong toward the train. As they galloped through the desert, the wind ripped across his face. Hidalgo felt alive again. Like when he still had all of his teeth and his back didn't ache every waking moment. Like before he'd given up his old ways and accepted the life of an old ranch hand in his home country.

Hidalgo knew they didn't belong in this time. Their brand of mischief was archaic, suited for a crueler world. They were creatures from a bygone era best put to pasture. He could see it now. A new age of marvels and miracles awaited, and men like him were not part of that equation. And it was probably for the best. In his heart, he knew this would be their last ride together, win or lose.

The men lined up their horses along the broad side of the first passenger car. The train—a locomotive anchored by four passenger cars, a single boxcar, and a caboose—chugged across an empty stretch of track along the Mojave Desert. Besides the Calico Mountains and the mining town that carried their namesake, nothing existed out here for miles. The only witnesses to their transgressions this night would be half-starved coyotes and God himself.

A furious gust swept across the valley, chilling Hidalgo's bones. The warm amber glow radiating from the kerosene lamps swaying in the windows looked particularly inviting. One by one, the men struck their matches and lit their fuses. Hidalgo gently pressed off his stirrups, raising himself into a standing mount. He swung his left leg over the saddle and waited until his horse was level with the passenger car's entryway. He took a breath, timed his jump, and leapt over the gap. He clung to the railing and pulled himself up the narrow steps. Winded, he drew his revolver and waved the men over.

As each man clambered up, the horses fell away one by one, fading into a veil of dust and darkness until it was just them and the train.

Hidalgo nodded. Villareal and Thompson drew their revolvers. They kicked the door open and charged inside, screaming and waving their dynamite. Benson and Blackhawk followed next. Hidalgo and Emery brought up the rear.

The six of them stood there for what seemed an eternity, unblinking, unmoving.

Apart from the rattling of the car, the hissing of dynamite fuses was the only sound within its confines.

"Put those out," Hidalgo said, nodding at the dynamite in their hands. The men snuffed the fuses and gazed at the carnage.

A wealth of viscera painted the passenger car. The upholstery on the chairs was draped with organs and splattered with yellow fatty tissue. The carcasses of what were once men and women lay slumped on their seats and the floor, the rags of drenched clothing beside them nigh impossible to distinguish from shreds of meat.

Emery bent over, pulled his bandana down, and heaved on the floor.

"What in God's name happened here?" Villareal said, crossing himself.

"This is unnatural," Blackhawk said, kneeling beside the torso of a woman. Her lower half had been lost somewhere within the tangle of severed limbs decorating the car. With a gloved hand, he gently turned her trunk over flat on its stomach. Small serrations marked the length of her spine to the base of her skull.

Thompson removed his kepi. "Not during war have I seen something like this."

"Nitroglycerin," Hidalgo said. "I have seen the remains of exploded railroad workers like this when they hollow out the mountains."

"This ain't no explosives, Jefe," Emery said standing back up again. He wiped his mouth with the back of his hand. "The rest of the car is unscathed."

The men inspected the car. Walls, windows, the floor, all intact. Not so much as a splintered beam overhead.

"Someone beat us to the punch," Benson said. "A botched robbery."

Blackhawk shook his head. "Nothing botched about this. There is intent in this mayhem."

Hidalgo faced the hallway that coupled the next carriage. Darkness stretched down the train. Only small glints of moonlight pierced the windows, catching on the silhouettes of lifeless, bobbing heads. "The lanterns are all out. Whoever did this may still be here," Hidalgo said. "Toward the rear."

Thompson sighed and raised his revolver as he peered into the stretch of infinite black. "Shall we take a look, amigos?"

The men stared at one another in silence, faces pale.

Hidalgo nodded. "I'll go first, muchachos," he said, unhooking a lantern off the wall.

In silence, the six of them moved single-file down the narrow aisle toward the back of the train, their boots trudging over wet, creaking floorboards and shards of glass. Car after car, it was all the same: slumping piles of meat and blood; the flickering light of Hidalgo's lantern reanimating the departed as their shadows danced on the walls, mocking their passage.

A foul odor permeated the air toward the back of the train; a stench of rot and sulfur that burned the sinuses. Emery groaned and pulled the bandana over his face.

A trail of blood and excrement led directly to the last compartment. Hidalgo lifted the dimming lantern to the splintered door.

"Help me," a woman's voice called from within the boxcar.

He leaned forward and pressed his ear against the door.

"Help me!" cried a man's voice, this one louder.

He raised his pistol.

A cacophony of pleas erupted within. "Helpmehelpmehelpmehelpme!"

Hidalgo kicked the fractured door inward and charged inside, the rest of the men storming in behind him.

"Jesus Christ," Thompson said.

Within the lantern's faint glow, Hidalgo could scarcely discern what he was seeing. The floor, walls, and ceiling were besieged with inky, fluid movement. He brought the lantern to the nearest wall. A sea of arachnids the size of armadillos clambered over one another, their long, shelled legs the color of rust. Their carapaces were rocky and speckled like granite. Like stars, the lamplight shimmered off the multitude of black eyes dotting the top of their shells. At his boots, the things scurried fervently over the defiled remains of the passengers, their mandibles snapping through bone and meat. He jumped back, slamming into the men. Blackhawk caught and straightened him up.

"What in the hell are these things?" Emery said just as one dropped from the ceiling, smacking down in front of him.

The thing tilted its body upward and opened its mandibles. A small tongue-like appendage slid out from its maw. "Help me," it said in mimicry of a human voice. "Help me."

The swarm on the floor paused their feeding frenzy and followed its lead as they turned toward the men. Like feelers, they pushed out thin, fleshy tongues and waggled them up and down. "Helpmehelpmehelpmehelpme!"

"Aw, fuck!" Emery drew on the nearest one and fired a shot. The top of its shelled head exploded, sending up gray bits of meat. The thing collapsed, its legs uncurling limply at its sides.

In the shadows, something half hissed, half burbled. Hidalgo swung the lamp toward the source of the sound. A large head reared itself from the darkest depths of the boxcar. In appearance, it was like the others, only larger. Hidalgo surmised it was

94

on par with a large steer. This one was different though. Its rocky shell was marbled with silver veins. A few flayed strands of rope were still tied around its carapace. The thing's legs, gangly and rugged, pushed it forward.

"What is that?" the spider-thing said, its mandibles open as it thrust its tongue out. "What is that? What is that?"

"Holy shit," Benson said.

"Get back," Hidalgo said, waving them away.

"Load it on the train," the thing said. "Load it on the train. Load it on the train. Load it on the train."

The spider-thing lifted a long, pointed leg and thrust it at Hidalgo. Villareal grabbed him by the scruff of his coat and threw him toward the men. The leg came down on Villareal's chest with a resounding crack. The thing withdrew its leg, sending up a spurt of blood from the fresh cavity. Villareal offered a single gurgle before he began to topple forward. The spider-thing opened its mandibles and clamped them shut on his torso, splitting him in half.

"No!" Hidalgo screamed, hurling the lantern at the floor beneath the spider-thing's legs. The lantern smashed open. A swell of fire engulfed the floor, splitting the car in half and separating the men from most of the swarm. The spider-thing shrieked, the sound like iron scraping against iron.

The light of the raging flames revealed the extent of the horrors inside. The things were bigger in the light. Uglier. They were akin to something between a crab and a spider, their shells and craggy legs seemingly made of granite or limestone.

A swarm of the things began to drop from the walls and ceiling, scaling over each other on their path toward the men.

As the flames lapped up the corpses, miniature arachnids began to spawn from their remains, their tiny mandibles shearing through pale, rancid meat.

While it was distracted by the flames, Thompson opened fire on the large spider-thing, sparks flying where the bullets chipped at its rock-like exterior. Spurned by his courage, the rest of the men fired a volley at the gangly nightmare. The thing reeled and shrieked, swinging its two front legs across the air like scythes.

Amidst the fire and smoke, Hidalgo crouched and gripped Villareal by his bandolier, hauling him backward the way they came. He stopped when he noticed his friend's entrails unspooling on the floor.

A rough hand rocked Hidalgo's shoulder. "He's gone, Jefe," Blackhawk said. "We need to fall back!"

Hidalgo frowned and released his grip on Villareal. He stood and emptied his revolver into a pair of approaching spiders. Their shells ruptured as they toppled over, their legs curling in on themselves.

"Fall back!" Hidalgo yelled over the fire's roar and the crack of gunfire.

Thompson and Emery darted past the screen of smoke and back toward the passenger cars. Benson emptied his gun and followed close behind. Hidalgo shuffled backward as he reloaded his revolver. Blackhawk covered him, picking off some stragglers scurrying past the flames. Once the things stopped coming, Hidalgo and Blackhawk sprinted toward the first car.

Regrouping with the rest of the men, Hidalgo leaned against a wall and exhaled, his heart bumping against his chest like a piston. He slammed the butt of his pistol against the wall. It was his only way to fight the tears starting to pool under his eyes. He'd known Luis from their time in Guadalajara, deserters of the Mexican Army both fleeing to a new country in search of plunder and riches.

"What in the holy hell was that?" Benson said, his revolver trained on the hallway.

"I don't know," Hidalgo said, trying to compose himself. He sucked in a deep breath and felt the fire in his chest spread through his limbs. His body had protested every ounce of exertion.

"Spawn of the Devil," Blackhawk said, reloading. "Those things are not of our world."

The shrieks of the spider-thing had ceased as the fire continued to blaze inside the boxcar.

"We've gotta get out of here," Emery said. "I don't intend to end up torn to ribbons or slumpin' and swollen like these people." He peered over the remains of some of the still-intact passengers as their bellies bulged into their laps.

"The dead don't bloat so quickly," Hidalgo said, stepping away from the seats.

"He's right," Blackhawk said. "You all saw what came out of the bodies down there. Hatchlings. Swarms of them."

"They're going to reproduce soon," Thompson said.

"Well, fuck me," Emery said.

"Jefe," Thompson said. "We can make our way toward the locomotive and stop the train just like we planned. We'll get off and ride the hell out of here."

Hidalgo kept his eyes on the dead passengers, watching for any sudden movements. They had died horrible, undeserving deaths. What awaited humanity if those things were to escape? He took off his hat and ran a trembling hand through his moist, gray hair. He turned his hand over. It was wrinkled and mottled with liver spots, veins, and broken blood vessels. He thought about the creature's carapace, its rocky, speckled exterior. "That thing down there. It is old. Like us."

"What do you mean, Jefe?" Thompson said.

"They dug that thing up deep in the mountains, amigo. It must have been there for years. Dormant under all that rock. That thing is ancient. Prehistoric. Beyond the reach of time."

"What are you saying?" Blackhawk said.

"That its time has passed. Like ours. There is no room in this world for evil things like us anymore. We can't let it escape," Hidalgo said, turning to the men, his eyes sharp, focused, the fire of his youth returned. "Let it be the only good thing we've ever done."

The wind rattled the window panes. Hidalgo spared a glance and saw his reflection staring back. His face was a dry riverbed, carved out by wrinkles and scars. His beard had silvered like the veins on the spider-thing. *Not long left in this world*, he thought.

"I'm with you, Jefe," Blackhawk said. "Those things cannot be loosed upon the world."

"Life was gonna be downhill from here anyways, fellas," Benson said. "I'm with you."

"Shit," Thompson said. "I'll follow you hombres to the depths of Pandemonium itself."

Emery sighed and nodded. "What do you suggest?"

"We could derail the train," Thompson said. "Speed it up, stick some dynamite between the cranks and wheels…"

Hidalgo shook his head. "No. The creatures would flee into the desert and multiply. We have to destroy the train."

"Hell," Emery said. "How?"

"We have to move down this train and blow every car one by one. We make sure every corpse and creature is destroyed."

"Let's see," Thompson said. "We can uncouple the locomotive, leaving us six cars including the caboose. We have five sticks of dynamite amongst ourselves. Shit! We'll need Luis's stick."

A shriek reverberated down the entire length of the train. The men turned toward the boxcar where Villareal had fallen. A hoard of dark shapes scuttled toward them, dousing the flames with their bodies.

"Emery, Benson," Hidalgo said. "Uncouple the locomotive. We can't lead them to civilization. After that, we won't have long before the train comes to a stop. We'll need to blow the rest of the cars before they can escape."

Emery and Benson hurried to the front of the car, squatted, and lifted the coupling bolt that connected the locomotive to the rest of the train. They watched the backside of the tender car as the locomotive sped off into the night without them.

The rest of the train rolled forward on sheer momentum, its rattling beginning to slow.

Hidalgo drew his revolver as the wave of rolling blackness approached. "We fight together and move up together. Emery, light your fuse."

Emery lit his stick. Together, they moved up, crossing into the second car.

"I can't see a damn thing ahead of me," Benson said.

"Shoot at the darkness," Hidalgo said, stepping forward. He opened fire at the onrushing surge as it obscured every sliver of moonlight shining through the windows. Every gunshot lit the car for a fraction of a second, revealing the orgy of teeming terrors crawling across the train. The men at his back opened fire, sparks flying off the walls around them. The moisture of blood and brains misted the air, mixing with the odor of gunpowder and smoke.

In the pitch of the darkness, Hidalgo felt their spindly limbs brush against his legs. He stomped his boots, digging his spurs deep into their shells. Every crack urged him on, every shriek restored another year of his youth.

As soon as they reached the middle of the second car, Emery tossed his stick toward the farthest corner of the first carriage.

Hidalgo held his breath.

The explosion rocked the train, hurling everything and everyone into the ceiling. The men came down on the seats and floor, the impact knocking the breath from Hidalgo's lungs.

Darkness filled his world again. He offered a look at his back. The car was gone, blown open and exposed to the desert, the moonlight painting the empty remains of the car. What hadn't been destroyed outright was already ablaze.

A choking veil of smoke wafted through the carriage. The groans and hacking coughs of old men filled the car.

He pushed himself off the wet floor, the muscles in his arms and legs straining as they contracted. There came a quick sizzle and a new fuse lit the car, the creatures now partly visible in the flicker of its light.

"I got this one," Benson said. In the light, he looked weathered, tired, white dust caked his face. Like a ghost. "Keep it moving, fellas!"

The spiders, now scattered on the floor of the aisle, twitched before springing over onto their legs. "Helpmehelpmehelpmehelpme!"

"Shit!" Hidalgo said. "Move up!"

He ran. Some of the things not directly under his boots crawled back up the walls, their legs swiping at his arms, slicing through his coat and skin.

He aimed at one and fired. *Click.* Empty. No time to reload, he swung the butt of his revolver in a left-to-right arc, like a club. A few blows connected, shattering their heads, their brains spewing on his face. He kicked and swung his way through the third car, his men firing point blank into the terrors still lingering at his flank.

"Ahhh!" Benson cried out, his light barely afloat amidst a swarm of spiders already on top of him. By his side, Emery fired off the last of his ammunition before they cut him down, his silhouette dissolving into the obscurity of the floor. As Thompson and Blackhawk reached the third car, Benson's light sank into the carnivorous mound.

The blast at his back ripped the second car apart, the thunder booming across the train once more. The force of the explosion flung Thompson into Hidalgo's side, knocking his face into the back of a leather-padded seat. Blood and teeth poured freely from his mouth and down his chin.

"Goddamnit," Thompson said, the moonlight now settling on his own bloodied mouth. Thompson prodded the floor. "I can't find my gun."

Hidalgo checked for his own revolver, which was also lost.

"We have to keep moving," Blackhawk said, hooking an arm around each downed man's armpit. He lifted them, standing them against the wall. He retrieved a matchstick and lit his fuse. "Run," he said, dropping the stick at his feet before starting for the next car with a wounded gait.

Hidalgo sprinted past the pricking legs and snapping mandibles, Thompson at his heels. They leapt into the fourth car, scuttled into an empty nook to either side of an aisle, and took cover under a seat.

The car detonated, flinging the spiders in every direction. A downpour of wood and limbs and shells rained down on the desert floor.

Hidalgo pulled himself up, out from under the cover, wiping the dust from his eyes. As far as he could see, the darkness continued to roll toward them.

A never-ending nightmare. He peered around. Thompson was already up and lighting his fuse. Behind them, a trail of fire and debris and nothing else. Not even Blackhawk.

"Come on, Jefe," Thompson said, drawing his saber. "Almost there."

Thompson screamed as he stormed down the passenger car, swinging and hacking his way into the boxcar like a soldier leading a charge. The things screeched in the dark. His blade sliced through every leg and carapace it came into contact with, their shelled bits flying every which way. Hidalgo followed him, limping past the smoldering floor and into the ruins of the next carriage.

Inside, the walls and ceiling had nearly burned away along with most of the arachnids, which were no more than ashen rock. On the floor of the entryway, Villareal gazed at an open patch of starry desert sky.

The faint beams of moonlight piercing the perforated roof revealed the giant spider-thing to be gone. Past the cloud of smoke, the entire front face of the caboose had been torn open. Something large and hideous moved within the shadows of the car.

A chorus of shrieks came from their flank.

Thompson flung his stick back into the passenger car and dove onto the charred floor, covering his head. Hidalgo quickly reached into Villareal's bandolier, snagged his dynamite, and slid it into his belt. He then dropped and curled up beside Thompson. The detonation sent up a wave of searing heat, the vibration rocking the train off the track and sending it pummeling into the earth. The train careened and flipped over onto its side. Hidalgo felt himself being thrown into the air before hitting the ground, his body rolling over sharp thicket.

The iron horse screeched and moaned while it skidded along the dirt. Its burning frame uprooted several Joshua trees until it came to a stop.

Hidalgo screamed as he pushed himself off the cold desert floor. Like hot coals against his flesh, his left arm burned in the worst way. The skin from his palm had degloved down his elbow where he'd tried to break his fall. He tucked his arm against his belly just as the chill winds began to sting his open wound. He grimaced, limping past a cloud of dust. "Thompson?" he called out. "Where are you, mi amigo?"

He shuffled toward the boxcar, now a shattered pile of smoldering wood and mangled iron. What remained of Thompson jutted out from under the train's frame from the chest up, the rest of his body pinned under its massive weight. Hidalgo closed his eyes and heard the gravel on the ground tumble with the breeze. He wanted to say a prayer for his men, but no words came.

The familiar burble and clatter of the spider-thing's mandibles broke the silence somewhere in the vicinity.

"Thing's gotta be worth a fortune," the creature said somewhere beyond the veil of dust and ash. "Thing's gotta be worth a fortune."

Hidalgo turned away and retrieved his friend's saber, lying just out of the reach of his curled fingers. He shambled away from the wreckage hoping to get a clear view of the scene.

Once he put enough distance between himself and the train, he trekked up a slope that overlooked the chaos. From here the stars shimmered again, and the Joshua trees swayed softly under the moonlight. Below, the haze had swallowed up everything near the burning rubble. There were no discernable signs of movement.

Eastward, the sound of hard galloping approached. *The kid.* "Shit," Hidalgo grumbled.

"Help me!" the spider-thing yelled, its pointed legs emerging from the smoke. It crawled past the wreckage and scuttled east atop the train tracks. "Help me!"

A plume of dust hung in the air where the kid had been running the horses in the distance. Hidalgo stuck the saber in the ground and pulled a match from his belt. He struck it against the trunk of a Joshua tree and lit his stick.

"Hey," he called out. "Over here!"

The spider-thing stopped and turned toward Hidalgo.

Hidalgo flung the stick. The spider-thing swung a craggy leg, knocking the explosive out of the air. The dynamite detonated just up the track, spitting up dirt and fire.

The stomping of hoofs wasn't too far off now. The poor kid would have no chance.

"Damnit," Hidalgo said under his breath, wincing. The pain in his left arm began to spread through his body like a brush fire. What few teeth he had left began to chatter inside his skull. He didn't know anymore if it was from the cold or the pain. Or both.

He retrieved another match and hobbled toward the spider-thing. "Hey!" he called out. "Come get me. I killed your children. And you killed my friends."

The thing charged at him.

He stood there, his left arm tucked into his belly, his right holding a single match.

When it neared, the spider-thing raised a leg and speared Hidalgo through the solar plexus. He huffed as the air was extinguished from his lungs. The thing lifted him off the ground and pulled him toward its snapping mandibles. Where there had been stars, there were now black spots filling his eyes.

He struck the match against the thing's stony face and lowered it toward his belly, where Villareal's stick of dynamite lay in his left hand's trembling grasp. The fuse ignited, casting both their faces in a warm red light. Hidalgo smiled at the old thing, blood seeping from his gums. It was all there was left to do in the face of death.

The fuse burned down into the blasting cap. Before the light engulfed them both, Hidalgo thought one last time of his friends and felt peace at last. *We did it muchachos.*

Bad Dogs

She was in the thralls of a comedown when the sedan's innards sputtered and exhaled a dying gasp of vapor.

"Damnit." Melody rolled toward the side of the curb and popped the brakes. She wiped the sliver of snot running down her nose with the back of her hand and reached for her phone. Dead. Under the amber glow of the streetlamp, she found her charging cable crimped and stripped down to its bare wiring.

Melody leaned her head back as the rain fell on the windshield like a torrent of marbles. She looked through the rearview mirror. Mayra stirred in her booster seat, rubbing her eyes with her small brown hands. "Mami?"

"Everything's okay, mija," she mumbled. "Just gotta get in touch with Taylor." The world outside the windshield looked distorted and she couldn't get a bearing on where she was. She'd ended up in some seedy part of town judging from the concentration of liquor stores and rundown motels. Her fling of the month, Taylor, had given her crap directions in what promised to be a simple exchange of flesh for warm, liquid bliss.

Melody scratched the abscess on her arm and gazed at the apartments across the street hoping to spot any familiar landmarks. Above, occulted faces peered out from barred windows and parted curtains. She felt their eyes on her. Hungry. Perverse. The back of her neck tingled just thinking about it.

Swallowing a dry lump, Melody went around back and unsnapped Mayra from her booster seat. "We gotta go get help, mija." She bundled her daughter in a polyester blanket and held her close.

Heavy rains came down as she dashed through a cascade of dirty runoff and ducked under the awning of a boarded-up appliance store. Squinting, she was able to make out a sign on the corner across the street. Jefferson.

At the end of the block, a pair of men stumbled toward her, heads stooped, fidgety hands fumbling inside their jacket pockets. She clutched Mayra closer to her chest and started to walk the opposite way.

Mayra squirmed in her grasp as the rain pelted her round, smooth face. Melody looked back. The men continued to stride behind her. Her heartbeat quickened, knocking against her chest while she looked around for a friendly face or a passing car. Anyone she could flag down.

Nothing.

The street seemingly stretched forever and her thin arms began to ache as the weight of her three-year-old daughter became unbearable.

She turned again. The men were walking faster, closing in; their footfalls nearly shrouded by the spatter of rain.

Just past the empty parking lot of an auto parts store, she spotted an old telephone booth, its pale blue light like a beacon in the void. She shuffled inside, shifted Mayra onto one arm, and pressed the door shut with her free hand. The men sauntered drunkenly past, fading into the misty night.

Melody exhaled, pushed an old phone book aside, and planted Mayra down on the small counter beneath the payphone. She rubbed her arms as the hairs on her skin turned prickly from the cold. The scent of urine and copper lingered in the air but she decided to endure it until it was safe to go outside again.

It wasn't long before the glass started to fog from the warmth of her breath. Her trembling hand patted her back pocket for some smokes when she realized she'd left them in the car. It was just as well, with Mayra inside.

Her elbow bumped the side of the booth. It was cramped, like a filthy iron maiden. Four glass panels, a counter, and a payphone smudged with greasy fingerprints. She hadn't seen a phone booth like this in ages but she was glad she'd found it.

Not wanting to take any chances, she peered outside the glass, making sure the men hadn't doubled back. Nothing. Shaking her head, she started to wonder if she'd been overreacting again. She'd been so tethered to a lifetime of trauma she couldn't tell a harmless stranger from a monster. She stroked Mayra's cheeks and smiled. For both their sakes.

Her daughter raised her chubby fingers to her nose and scratched. "Mami, I, um, cold."

Melody adjusted the blanket around her daughter. "Everything is alright, bebita. We'll be at Taylor's soon. Mami just needs to get her medicine from him."

"I want Papi."

"Mami and Armando—I mean, Papi, don't talk anymore, mija. He's not very happy with me."

Just beyond the condensation and graffiti-etched glass, she thought she saw a flash of movement across the street. She wiped away a film of moisture and peered through the glass. Directly below the flickering light of a lamppost, elongated fingers reached out from the darkened maw of an alley, their long, curved nails scraping against a brick wall.

"What the f—"

A small glint of light shimmered not more than twenty feet to her left. There, what appeared to be pointed teeth protruded from a long canid head as it skulked in the rain. Yellow gleaming eyes jutted from its sunken face, observing her there all alone in the booth beside her tiny human.

Something tapped the pane behind her. She shuffled around in the confines of the booth. The vague, abhorrent forms of two bipedal things leaned against the door, their ribs protruding from mangy bellies. Their gnarled, clawed hands scraped down the glass. *Screeee.* Melody quickly braced the door with her shoulder.

"Mami," Mayra said, pointing outside. Two veiled shapes zipped across the fogged panes. "Bad dogs."

"Yes, baby," she muttered, her lips quivering. "Everything is going to be okay."

What the hell was happening? What was she seeing? She shut her eyes until they hurt, hoping the visions would go away.

Something pushed against the glass. She pushed back and leaned against the door. Within moments, the panes had completely frosted over, obscuring the world outside.

Mayra began to cry.

There came a cacophony of muffled growls that almost sounded like broken, guttural speech. Then came the wild yipping and panting.

"Mami," Mayra said, sniveling now. "Scary dogs."

Pressure built up behind Melody's eyes and a wave of nausea started in her head and swept through her body. She pressed her lips together and held down the surge of hot bile coming up her throat. A trickle of tears streamed down her cheeks and down her neck mingling with the rainwater.

Another push at the door. Stronger this time. She planted her feet and pushed back with outstretched arms, the weight of her entire body bracing the door. Her muscles strained, burning as she pushed.

After a moment, the pushing ceased and there was a lull in the growling. She quickly shoved a hand in her pocket, fishing for anything she could use as a weapon. Her fingers grazed a couple of quarters. She turned to look at the phone. Of course. "You idiot," she said under her breath. She pulled the change out of her pocket and slipped fifty cents through the coin slot.

She unhooked the phone from its cradle. Her index finger hovered over the 9 before she pulled it back. Calling the cops was out of the question. How would she explain that a junky and her three-year-old daughter had been surrounded by a pack of werewolves inside a phone booth? No one would ever believe her.

"I want Papi," Mayra said, sobbing uncontrollably now.

"No, mija. We need Taylor. He's not far from here. He can help us." Melody punched in Taylor's area code. She caught sight of her smeared, warped reflection on the chrome telephone box. Dark, tired eyes stared back, snot dripping down her nose. And the track marks. She ran two fingers along the intersecting scars and collapsed veins blemishing her arms. Her fingers then traced the raspberries on her chest where countless cigarettes had been forcibly extinguished through the years. She'd been nothing but a human pincushion. A prop for a revolving door of malicious suitors. Predators, all of them.

"Mami?" Mayra's eyes had reddened and welled with tears. Her daughter was a splitting image of Melody at the same age. An untainted reflection of smooth, clean skin, a soul uncorrupted by abuse and dubious decisions.

Melody hung up and punched in Armando's number. The phone rang as the yipping continued. The call went to voicemail.

"Armando?" she said. "This is Melody. I'm with Mayra. Listen, my car broke down and I need you to pick us up. We're somewhere on Jefferson by an auto parts store. Armando? Please hurry." She hung up.

Melody lifted Mayra and brought her toward her chest, rocking her gently as she hummed *Tu Tu Teshcote*, an old Mexican lullaby her mother had sung to her. The warmth of Mayra's body spread to her own, radiating outward from her chest to her limbs.

Outside, the monsters' yipping reached a crescendo, their piercing whines wrecking her eardrums. Mayra wept uncontrollably, her face flushed and hot. Melody pressed Mayra's head against her heart and continued to hum the lullaby, louder now so that she drowned out the monsters outside. Over and over, she hummed the tune until the sound of tires rolling over asphalt washed away their shrieks. When she opened her eyes, twin beams of light cut through the darkness as Armando's car pulled up along the curb.

The things were gone. Cautiously, Melody stepped outside and surveyed the street while she hoisted Mayra up on her shoulders. Across the way, a dead tree swayed in the breeze, its gangly limbs scraping against an alley wall. A pair of malnourished dogs ambled up the street, sniffing discarded sandwich wrappers caught in the gutters.

Inside Armando's car, a wave of warm air greeted mother and daughter. Armando nodded, smiled, and reached a hand out to Mayra who curled her small fingers around his. They drove off in silence.

Melody offered her side view mirror a glance. Just outside the glow of the phone booth's light, an upright silhouette watched the car roll down the street. Melody looked away. She wasn't sure what was real anymore. The scars on her body would have to be proof enough. Monsters, men, it made no difference; in this world, the hungry would always prey on the vulnerable. She wiped Mayra's tears as she planted her on her lap, vowing to make sure her daughter would never be amongst them.

Birthday Boy

Kiko looked upon the field of blue agave, the sun in his eyes as Pancho's red truck rolled down the narrow dirt road. His father placed a hand on his shoulder and squeezed, smiling while his jimador returned from a long day harvesting what Kiko always thought looked like big pineapples.

But Kiko knew better now that he was older. Tomorrow he'd be turning ten, and already his father had ensured he'd learned as much about the distillery as possible.

Men have to learn to take care of their business.

Pancho pulled into the estate's driveway, grinning, his face dark and leathery from toiling under the sun all those years. "Don Ernesto," he said, tipping his hat.

Kiko's father embraced his old friend. "Panchito, how was the haul?"

"Good, Jefe," he said, retrieving his coa from the truck. The pole's tip had a round blade that was used to hack away the thick leaves from the piña, the core of the agave. "A few more trucks are on the way. Today was a scorcher, though."

"I'm sure," his father said. "That reminds me. Did you have time to get the thing I asked for?"

"Of course." Pancho walked to the flatbed and retrieved a donkey piñata, its bright tinsel ribbons fluttering in a warm breeze. "I found an old merchant in town selling these."

"Perfect," his father said, handing Pancho a rolled wad of cash.

"Excited for the big day tomorrow, Kiko?" Pancho said, patting his arm. The man smelled of coffee, sweat, and tequila, the scents Kiko had come to associate with adulthood and hard work. With being a man.

"Yes, Pancho."

"I'm glad. I'll see you two later, I've got to unload my haul before I stuff that donkey with candy."

Before his father ushered him back inside the hacienda, Kiko smiled.

It was late when he heard murmuring downstairs. Kiko vaulted off the side of the bed and peeked down the stairwell. His father, alongside Pancho and a pair of men gathered by the door, all of them tucking pistols into their waistbands.

His father always told him the guns were necessary to protect the distillery from rivals in the area. Jalisco was crawling with bad men, like scorpions hiding beneath rocks.

"Vámonos," Kiko heard his father say before they scurried out the door. Eventually, the sound of trucks faded into the night.

Kiko jumped back into bed and switched off the light. He wondered if Pancho would bring his family to the party tomorrow. He'd been shy around his daughter, Patti, but she made him feel good inside. Maybe he'd finally gather enough courage to ask her to join him on the jumper. He even considered letting her get the first crack at the piñata.

He closed his eyes, nestling his head into his pillow as he waited for sleep to find him. Before he dozed off, a deep moan bellowed through the house.

"Unghhhhhhh," the sound echoed, long and strained, like the time Pancho severed one of his fingers chopping agave and the maid shrieked in terror at the sight of all the blood.

It came again. "Unghhhhhhh." It sounded like it came from deep within the house. Kiko placed his hands over his ears.

After a few minutes, the sound ceased. He didn't hear gasping or footsteps or cries for help. There was only the sound of crickets chirping outside his window and nothing else.

He pulled his bedsheets over his face and shut his eyes until they hurt. Eventually, sleep came for him.

Kiko handed Patti the stick, his smile crooked. He blushed as she smiled back.

His father winked at him from across the yard, raising his beer bottle high.

Pancho slipped the blindfold over his daughter's eyes and gently guided her near the piñata as the crowd gathered.

The piñata had been hoisted over an old juniper tree where Kiko had carved his initials long ago.

Patti took a swing at the colorful donkey. Pancho tugged the rope causing the piñata to jerk upward.

Near the open bar, the banda played corridos, the music rumbling through Kiko's body.

Patti swung again. Another miss.

He thought he heard a whimper as the piñata reeled in the air, not unlike the strung-up street dogs he'd seen swaying on lampposts back in town. His father told him some people in this world were cruel. Without remorse.

Patti took another hack. This one connected. A large gape in the piñata's side offered up a wealth of candy, spilling like little guts.

Patti removed her blindfold, smiled at him, and dove for the candy.

It was a good birthday.

His father planted a soft kiss on his head, waking him.

"I've got something urgent to tend to. I won't be long."

"Alright," Kiko said, squinting at his father's silhouette as it disappeared behind the door. Again, his father took some men and left.

The shadows from the juniper's gnarled, swaying limbs crept past the window and danced on his wall, so he rolled onto his side and thought about Patti. She had thanked him and hugged him before leaving with Pancho and the family. Maybe he would ask his father to set up another horseback excursion with their families sometime.

He nearly drifted into sleep when that familiar sound roused him as it echoed across the house. "Unghhhhhhh," the voice groaned.

"Hello?" Kiko called out. "Who's out there?"

No answer came for some time. But he was sure he'd heard it, somewhere in the house with him.

Men have to learn to take care of their business.

He sat up, took a deep breath, and made his way downstairs. No one in the hallway. Not even in the nooks behind the storage trunks or within the shadows of the coat racks.

Perhaps it had been the hacienda's ancient bones creaking in protest to the wind. As if in reply, the groaning came again, the sound directly under his feet. The basement.

He balled his fists and ambled past the wooden door and down the old stone steps. He yanked on the lightbulb's chain and looked around. The room was littered with junk: old farming equipment, spools of stained rope, rusty scythes, vintage sombreros hanging on the walls.

Soft wheezing emanated from the dirty table near the back where Pancho kept his tools. There, under the glow of faint light, his donkey piñata lay on its side, its belly slowly rising and falling as if gasping for air. The gape in the cardboard at its ribs looked wet and moldy, like necrotic tissue.

Kiko stepped back. "What are you?"

"I don't know! I don't know anything!" the piñata said.

Kiko's heart thumped inside his chest.

"Please, make the pain stop," the piñata said in short gasps, its breath rustling the paper ribbons beside its mouth.

The air in the basement was cool and Kiko felt the hairs on his arms turn prickly. "I can't help you."

"Please, it hurts so much."

Dark blotches filled his sight. He leaned against the wall, wanting to sit down, to catch his breath in the worst way. He was dreaming. He had to be. "No, this isn't real, you're just a piñata, you'll see." Kiko shoved his hand inside its cavity, his fingers probing for loose candy. Instead, he felt only damp mush drip down his knuckles. "There's no candy here."

The piñata's breaths became labored, shallower. "I don't know where the stash is. I swear. Please. Kill me."

"I-I can't," Kiko said. Warm tears pooled under his eyes, shrouding the world in a white haze.

The donkey spasmed on the table, a stream of melted chocolate oozing from its sides.

It wasn't real, he thought. Just a piñata. Shut it up, make it stop talking. He wiped away his tears, unhooked the coa hanging on the wall, and shuffled back to the paper-mâché donkey. It mouthed something, but no words came.

He lifted the pole in the air and brought it down on the piñata's neck, severing its head.

Kiko buried his face between his knees, sobbing until warm snot dripped down his chin. After some time, he heard tires rolling over gravel in the driveway.

He secured the coa on the wall, ran upstairs, and dove into bed.

Downstairs, the familiar affairs of night began to play out as they always had: the scents of coffee, sweat, and tequila; the sounds of boots stamping, of screaming men being dragged to the basement; the customary conversations between his father and strangers echoing through the old walls.

I don't know anything. Please, make the pain stop. I don't know where the stash is. Please. Kill me.

Kiko pulled the bedsheets over his face and closed his eyes until they hurt. He thought about Patti and the way she made him feel good inside. For a moment, it was enough to mute the screams.

The House of Laments

Rodrigo pulled off the highway and turned onto a narrow country lane just as snow began to pelt the windshield. The sedan bounced over a stretch of uneven road. Julia felt the baby kick and placed a hand over her belly.

"Sorry," Rodrigo said, "I'll drive slow."

Julia looked at her baby bump. She had never gotten this far before, and not for lack of trying.

"Don't worry," he said. "Things will be different. The doctor said so. The baby—Alma—is looking healthy."

"Yeah," she said, glancing out the window. The snow started to come down, dusting the countryside. The clouds had blotted out the sun, leaving the sky a mottled watercolor painting. It was a far cry from California.

Off the road, a hand-painted sign jutted crookedly from a patch of dead earth. *Estate Sale. End of the Road.*

"There it is," Rodrigo said. "We're heading the right way."

After a mile, they pulled up to a run-down homestead nestled on a vacant farm, its soil under an inch of fresh powder. The broken stems of dead corn stalks pierced the snow for miles in every direction.

There wasn't much to look at other than a rusted silo, a decrepit house, and a thicket of spruce and elm trees stretching aways back.

There were already trucks lined up on either side of the road, their flatbeds loaded with boxes and roped-down furniture. Rodrigo found parking alongside a fencepost near an old mailbox with a weathervane poking out the top.

Julia peered through the windshield. She wasn't used to houses like this in Los Angeles. Her whole life she'd yearned for a taste of the rural, the quiet that couldn't be found anywhere else but middle America. After the miscarriages, she knew the move to South Dakota would do them both good. Since they both worked from home, it wouldn't be a hindrance to their careers.

"Something sad about this place," Julia said, her gaze fixed on the farmhouse.

"Write about it in another one of your books," Rodrigo said looking out with her. "Maybe it's haunted."

She nodded blankly. The house, though charming in its own way, was in shambles. Even from inside the car, Julia could see the effects time and the elements had inflicted on its bones; the rotting clapboards and peeling paint left the house with a dirty, gray façade. Even the black curtains hanging over the windows were ragged and woeful. It stood as a corpse long picked clean by prairie scavengers.

Rodrigo helped Julia trudge up a creaky set of stairs and past the porch. A woman in a peacoat stood at the door. She waved her clipboard and smiled.

"Hello," she said, "and welcome to the Martin estate sale. Feel free to look around. Everything is marked and priced to sell."

"What happened to the previous owner?" Rodrigo said, bluntly, as he removed his gloves.

The woman lowered her clipboard, the cheer wiped from her face. "Well, Mr. Phineas Martin vanished a few years ago and was recently declared dead. Having no next of kin, the county possessed his property and is selling his belongings before the place is condemned."

"Condemned?" Julia asked.

"Yup. The house is in disarray and the terrain isn't good for farming anymore. The county thinks it'll be easier to vacate the land and fence it off rather than try selling it. Now, please, go and have a look." She half-shooed them into the house as more people began to make their way up the porch.

As Julia shuffled inside the living room, the floorboards creaked and bowed slightly under her shoes. The room was almost bare, save for a few rickety chairs and the fireplace mantle full of assorted trophies and porcelain figurines.

She wrinkled her nose. The house smelled of old newspapers, coffee, and stale cigarettes. And rot. A wet, foul stench she couldn't pinpoint.

She did her best to ignore the smell as Rodrigo reached out and squeezed her hand. He'd been doing his best to comfort her these last few months. She shook the memories and buried them deep inside as they came upon an office. A cherrywood desk sat toward the back of the room, almanacs and encyclopedias spread on its surface. Behind the desk there was a lone window draped in thick, black cloth, most of which was covered in a thin layer of dust and cobwebs. A sliver of daylight pierced the curtains and caught on a large corkboard hanging on the wall. It was pinned with faded pictures of missing children clipped from the backs of junk mail letters and newspapers. The most recent was from ten years prior, a missing four-year old girl from just outside town.

"Breaks my heart," a gruff voice said behind them, giving Julia's heart a jolt. An old man dressed in jeans and a plaid long-sleeve shirt leaned against the doorframe. His tired eyes scanned the corkboard with what Julia regarded as pity. "Mabel never could have kids and after she was killed, Phineas took to searching for missing children as a way to cope. Lord knows we have our share of runaways 'round these parts. I'm sorry," he said, reaching a hand out, "My name's Frank Hess. I was their neighbor for forty years. I live on the next farm over."

"Rodrigo and Julia Ortega," Rodrigo said, shaking Frank's hand. "Frank, you said Mabel was killed. Mind if I ask?"

Julia elbowed Rodrigo in the ribs.

Frank bit his lip and his eyes rolled upwards as if plumbing the depths of his mind. "It's been about twenty years now. They were on vacation in the Yucatan Peninsula, and, well, Phineas thinks she was mauled by a jaguar." Frank curled his fingers around his neck. "Poor Mabel's throat was ripped out and Phineas barely survived himself. Says he was blindsided by the thing, so no one quite knows what killed her, truth be told."

"Jesus," Julia said. She ran two fingers along her throat. A shiver ran up her spine.

"Yup," Frank said, crossing his arms. "The poor man was never the same after that. He'd already been suffering from dementia, but that just put the nail in the coffin. Phineas rarely left the house after he got back. Just kept to himself until he vanished. I think the poor bastard lost his senses one night, wandered off, and got himself dead. Probably exposure. Lots of prairie out there."

"I hear that," Rodrigo said.

"Well, I'll let you folks rummage around." Frank eyed Julia's belly and winked. "Nice meeting you three."

"Fucking terrible," Rodrigo said. "Maybe this house *is* haunted."

Julia nodded and left the office. They turned into a narrow hallway, and she ran a hand along the brittle wallpaper, her fingers collecting dust and flakes of paper.

There was grief within the walls as if a lingering soul weeping within. "I feel sorry for the both of them. Just tragedy after tragedy."

They stepped into the master bedroom and Julia flicked on the light. The window at the opposite end of the room had been boarded up. Fine shards of broken glass twinkled like diamonds beneath the windowsill. The mattress had already been stripped off the frame, leaving a thin metal skeleton in the center of the room. Something about the sight filled Julia with sorrow. How many nighttime conversations were had in this room? How many dreams were born? Now it had all been dismantled, sold off to strangers.

Rodrigo had told her she suffered from an *abundance of empathy*. Right or wrong, she tried not to let the thought get to her. Only two nightstands remained on either side of the frame. Julia walked over to the nearest one and opened a drawer. Her hands pawed around in darkness until she touched something slim and solid. She pulled out a vintage Kodak disposable camera. The kind her parents had used in the '90s on summer vacations when she was a little girl.

"What you got there?" Rodrigo said.

"It's an old-school camera," she said, flipping it over. "There's no tag on it."

"Does it work?"

"Let's see," she said, peering through the viewfinder. She centered Rodrigo's face and pressed the shutter release. The camera snapped and flashed.

"Hey!" Rodrigo said, rubbing his eyes. "Little warning next time?"

"Still good," she said, spinning a small dial on the camera. "Let's get a selfie."

"Sure, babe." Rodrigo squeezed beside her and made himself small as she raised the camera above their heads. They pressed their cheeks together and smiled. Julia pressed the release again. The camera clicked and flashed.

"That was it. Last one."

"That takes me back," Rodrigo said. "Haven't seen one of those in ages. I wonder if the pictures came out alright."

"I'm curious as to what kind of pictures the old man has in here. The poor guy didn't even have any next of kin." Julia frowned. She turned the camera over. Her warped reflection stared back from the lens. "Whatever memories he had in here are gonna end up in the trash. As if he never existed. So damn sad."

"Let's buy it," Rodrigo said, placing a hand on her shoulder. "We'll get them developed and go through them all. We'll make an evening of it. I'm sure Mr. Martin wouldn't mind."

Julia didn't know why but she loved the idea. The thought of exploring a stranger's memories had kindled something in her she couldn't explain. A longing for a past that wasn't hers, and one she had private access to. It would be almost like bringing back someone from the dead.

They asked the woman up front about the camera and she said it must have been an oversight. She charged them ten dollars. Rodrigo paid in cash. Julia didn't even bother exploring the kitchen toward the back of the house. She'd gotten all she needed from this place. As they drove back into town, she clutched the camera to her chest like a little girl with a new book, its secrets awaiting her.

"Let's find a photo lab," she said. As they pulled away from the house, she allowed herself to smile. For the first time in a long time, it was genuine.

They'd found a place in town that still developed film photography. Rodrigo joked these days it was akin to some archaic proto-science like alchemy. Julia didn't think he was far from the truth.

After they'd dropped off the film roll, they had gotten to unpacking and settling in. Rodrigo assembled a crib in the master bedroom in between website development gigs for his clients back in L.A. Julia set up an office in the corner of the living room and got the cylinders firing on her new romance novel in between the sporadic contractions.

The phone rang two weeks later on a late Tuesday afternoon. The shop had their photos ready. Julia had thrown herself into her new novel and had almost forgotten about them.

Rodrigo drove to pick up the photos and came back with a bottle of sparkling grape juice.

"I know you can't drink so here's the closest thing," he said, pouring them each a glass. He lay the envelope on the coffee table and flashed a smile. They nestled into the couch and pulled a blanket over their laps.

"You ready?" Rodrigo said, tipping his glass to hers.

"Yeah," she said. "To Mr. and Mrs. Martin."

She grabbed the envelope and slid out a stack of about two dozen glossy 5x7 prints.

The first print was an overexposed picture of a middle-aged woman, smiling as she clutched her purse in front of the Disneyland Monorail, scores of families jockeying behind her for a seat. She had bushy blonde hair and wore an oversized Minnie Mouse sweater, powder blue jeans, and white tennis shoes.

"She's dressed like my grandma did in the '80s," Rodrigo chuckled.

Julia flipped the picture over. "There's no timestamp."

"You're thinking digital pictures, babe," he said before sipping from his glass.

She slipped the photo at the back of the stack. The next picture was of a clear, blue lake. In it, a lanky green-eyed man with a warm smile sat on a small boat, his knees jutting out as he waved at the camera with one hand and gripped a fishing pole with his other.

"Cute," Julia said.

Then came pictures of birthdays at the park; candid shots of Phineas and Mabel at home, or toiling on the farm; photos of them, older now, holding each other as they leaned against a station wagon at the Grand Canyon.

"Look at that one," Rodrigo said, jabbing his finger on the print. "This must be the place where it happened."

It was a snapshot of Mabel sitting on the bottom step of a steep Mayan pyramid, the jungle canopy shrouding the sun as it fell below the horizon. The trees and fronds seemed to encroach upon Mabel as she sat, her hands clasped on her lap.

"I know this place," Julia said. Her finger traced the crumbling steps of the temple as it tapered into the sky. "This is the Nohoch Mul pyramid."

"Huh?"

"It's in Coba in the Yucatan Peninsula. I've read up on this place. In one of my books, my characters meet on vacation here. Most of the city is still buried underground, lost to time. They've only rediscovered a small portion of it."

"Wild," Rodrigo said, pouring himself another glass. "Wonder what kind of weird things are hidden down there."

Julia pulled out the next picture. It was a snapshot of an elm tree, the stars, like tiny white pinholes, barely visible in the expansive dark blue sky behind it.

"Hm," she said, "looks like Mabel is gone by this point."

Rodrigo pursed his lips and nodded. "Poor woman. Makes you wonder what attacked her."

Julia pulled up another picture; a blurred image of a porch, lit only by the fading light of the sun, which had now mostly sunk behind the plains. It appeared to be the same porch she'd labored to climb at the estate sale.

Another photo: an anonymous rural road at night as it vanished into a horizon where land met stars.

"Weird," Rodrigo said.

The rest were pictures of empty rooms, dark cellars, boarded windows, liminal spaces; even one of an out-of-focus phone booth at night, the distorted light of the flash bouncing off a wet street she thought she recognized from town.

"This doesn't make sense," Julia said. "These pictures are aimless and dark, washed out, fuzzy."

"Remember," Rodrigo said, knocking back the last of his drink, "the man had dementia. It had probably spiraled out of control by this point."

There was a final picture. Like everything before, it was dark, but Julia made it out to be a kitchen. There was an old gas stove with small, soiled rags littering a shadowed section of floor beneath it. And that was it.

She finally came upon the last two pictures they'd taken two weeks prior, clean and clear.

Rodrigo scooched close. "Hey, those came out great!"

"Wait a minute," Julia said, pulling back the last picture. Something caught her eye. "What does that look like to you?" She brought her fingernail to the tiny spot where the rags had been strewn below the stove.

Rodrigo took the picture and brought it close to his face, squinting. "That looks like clothing. Children's clothing." He handed the picture back. "But didn't Frank say Mabel couldn't have kids? When do you think this picture was taken?"

"Hard to say," Julia said, her eyes focusing hard on that tiny, shadowed spot. It did indeed appear to be clothing. She swore she could make out a small skirt with a dull pink striped pattern. Another article looked like a toddler's collared shirt.

"Why would he have children's clothing?" Rodrigo asked.

"The pictures on the corkboard. What if he wasn't looking for those kids? What if he's the reason they disappeared?"

"You mean those photos on the board were his collection?" Rodrigo shook his head. "No. Can't be. I think we're tired and letting our imaginations create boogeymen that don't exist." He stood and walked to the bedroom. "Come on, let's get some sleep. It's late and we're losing our minds."

"Yeah," Julia said, sliding the prints back in the envelope. "Guess you're right."

119

That night, the terrors found her as she slept. In her dream, she was tormented by the wails of children trapped inside a house. Their faces were obscured in a web of shadows behind a window as their tiny fingers clawed against glass. Something loomed over the sky, something great and terrible as it eclipsed the world. Then, she felt cold fingers sliding up her neck.

Julia bolted awake, the nightgown moist and clinging to her body. She placed a hand on her belly and massaged it in a slow, concentric motion.

Outside, a fresh snowstorm ravaged the house as the branches scraped against the bedroom window.

"Rodrigo?" Julia rocked Rodrigo awake.

"Hm?"

"We need to go back to that house."

"What?"

"I have to make sure. I-I can't shake this feeling that Phineas had something to do with those kids."

"Babe," Rodrigo mumbled. He looked out the window at the violent flurry frosting the window. "It's late. Give it a rest. The old man's dead and this is all in your head."

"I just need to check for those clothes, that's all. I think about Alma, if she were to go missing, I'd want to know. Please?"

Rodrigo regarded her for a moment. "You're serious?"

Julia looked at her belly again and nodded.

Rodrigo frowned, threw on his jacket, and strapped on his boots.

The trek back to the house had been slow as the wind rocked the car. The rural roads had already accumulated three inches of snowfall and the sedan's tires labored to slog through it all.

When they rolled in, they parked directly in front of the house, the car's headlights cutting through the night like a knife. The house had amassed a layer of snow and resembled a phantom rising from the frosted plains.

"Alright," Rodrigo said, reaching into the glove compartment. He retrieved a cheap plastic flashlight, its batteries clacking around inside like loose bones. "Let's go."

He'd left the car's engine running, the headlights guiding their way up the porch. Rodrigo tried the doorknob. When that didn't work, he pressed his shoulder against the frame and pushed. The latch and frame split apart and the door swung open.

Rodrigo flicked on the flashlight and threw the light around the living room. Motes of dust and snow from outside mingled in the air wherever the cone of light swayed. The house was considerably emptier now as if ransacked by thieves. All that remained were bundles of old newspapers stacked along the wall.

Julia retrieved the envelope from her coat and brought up the picture. "Let's just get a quick look under the stove and we'll leave."

The kitchen was toward the back of the house. It was cramped, old. Nothing but a pantry, a counter, and dilapidated cabinets. The faint light from the sedan's beams cast their shadows over an antiquated stove, creating a large dark spot in the center of the room.

Julia looked over the image again. The rags were sticking out of the shadows directly beneath the stove, which was slightly elevated off the ground. A cold draft swept in, raising the hairs on the back of her neck.

"Down there," she nodded toward the stove.

Rodrigo sighed as he got on his knees. He aimed the flashlight under the stove.

Julia moaned as she backed against the counter. She dropped the envelope and wrapped her arms around her belly while fluid seeped down her jeans and shoes, pooling on the floor. "It's happening," she groaned.

"Shit," Rodrigo said, jumping upright. He caught her arm and eased her onto the floor. "I won't be able to get us to the hospital in time with that snowstorm. We're gonna have to do this here."

Julia broke into short, labored breaths, the contractions tearing at her insides, the pain sweeping through her body like fire.

"We're gonna do this together, baby."

Rodrigo quickly removed her shoes and pants and squeezed her hand.

The snow began to blow inside the kitchen, flying into her skin like frigid daggers.

She pushed, feeling her muscles expand and contract, her fingers wound tight around Rodrigo's hand.

"I see her head," Rodrigo said. "Keep push-"

A naked man emerged from the shadows at Rodrigo's back. As he shambled into the light Julia gasped at the sight of his pale body, lanky and gaunt, his ribs protruding from a thin film of skin like a malnourished animal. Before she could warn him, the man plunged his teeth into Rodrigo's throat. The pallid man whipped his head to the side and ripped out a chunk of bloody flesh. Rodrigo slumped lifelessly to the floor, his flashlight plunking beside him, its light spinning until it settled on a puddle of blood, now expanding around his body.

"No, God, no!" Julia shrieked, her body still in the throes of giving birth.

The naked man dropped to his knees and lapped from the crimson pool. When he finished, he staggered toward Julia. He bent over her, his pungent breaths shallow and quick as blood seeped down his chin and chest. In the light of the car's beams, she made out the familiar green eyes from the photos.

Phineas' eyes settled on the envelope before his long fingers plucked it off the floor. He sifted through the pictures as his eyes widened and his brows arched, his face painted with the look of pain and familiarity, of things remembered. Thin lips curled to reveal twin spear-like fangs. Then, his mouth twisted into something vaguely resembling a smile.

Julia sobbed as she made her final push. Her daughter slipped onto the floor at her mother's feet, small arms flailing as her wails echoed throughout the empty house.

"Please, don't hurt us," Julia whispered as she tried to sit up.

Phineas stooped, reached out a hand, and slid a long-nailed finger across Julia's neck.

Julia gargled as warm blood spewed from the open wound at her throat and plopped down the sides of her neck. She reached a hand to Alma who was still tethered to her. Phineas followed Julia's gaze and tilted his head. He hunched over the child and severed the umbilical cord with a swipe of his fingernails.

Phineas scooped Alma off the floor and cradled her in the crook of a long, bony arm, their bodies bathed in yellow light.

Hearing the cries of her daughter sent a swell of blood rushing to her head. Julia felt a surge of warm, stinging tears as her heart knocked inside her chest. She wanted to scream and tear off the old man's face. Instead, she felt the rage seep out from her throat until there was only lethargy.

Phineas crouched low to the floor and scuttled under the oven, baby and pictures in tow, all vanishing into the shadows within.

Julia heard the creak of what may have been the hinges of a cellar door swinging open. Deep within the bowels of the house, the cries of children slithered up through the floorboards before they were muffled by the howling wind.

Dark spots filled Julia's eyes as the skin on her body grew cold and numb as if she were melding into the frigid floor itself. Outside, the car's headlights flickered as the snowstorm continued to rage through the night.

Caravan

Rudy raised his arm and wiped the sweat from his brow. Around him, thousands of people from the caravan settled into the Zocalo in Mexico City. Here and there, volunteers wove their way through the crowd, dispensing food, medical aid, and clothes.

A light-skinned boy named Enrique who'd travelled in Rudy's immediate clique received a pristine *Cruz Azul* cap from a generous woman. She caressed his face and made friendly chatter with his father Guillermo, the fat man from Honduras. Rudy looked at his own arms. They were dark, and shimmering with sweat. A group of curious onlookers gave them cold stares as if looking upon a herd of animals.

Rudy's mother pulled him close. "Mijo, stay close. Stray children have been known to get snatched here."

Rudy turned his head to look up at her.

"This world is full of monsters. They kidnap children and demand ransoms or sell their organs on the black market. We're not in Guatemala. People disappear here all the time."

"Monsters?" Rudy asked. He wanted to ask what she meant but he knew better than to question his mother.

They walked inside a large tent and received the best meal he'd had in weeks since crossing the border into Chiapas: A bowl of rice, beans, corn, and tortillas.

"Enjoy," his mother said. "It only gets harder from here."

The nights were the worst for Rudy. He sat alone, wrapped his arms across his chest, and shivered in front of the campfire. He looked at the people around him as the light danced across their bodies. Their faces looked gaunt and pale, like corpses. Many had grown thin, relying on the generosity of strangers for food. He'd spotted some of the men catching rats and bashing them against rocks and grilling them over the open flames.

Some of the older travelers stayed behind to wither away as their feet could no longer carry them.

Tonight, they camped outside of San Miguel, Sinaloa. His mother had left for town to scavenge for dinner. She often left him alone at night as she offered her services to old townsfolk or to local butchers who detested cleaning the bloody counters in return for whatever scraps they could part with.

As he waited for his mother to return, he made a game of counting the people in his clique. He counted fifty. The group had thinned out over the last month. Many of them disappeared during the night. Some, he'd overheard, had turned back as the trip dragged on and food became scarce. Others sought asylum in the small towns they'd ventured through, choosing to start anew in Mexico. Sometimes he'd even hear parents crying on about their children vanishing, pleading for anyone to help start a search party. Most people ignored the pleas and carried on. That's why his mother didn't let him make friends with any of the other children; it would hurt too much if he didn't see them again.

Rudy wondered about the monsters his mom had mentioned. They couldn't be real, could they?

He tried not to think about it. There was a rational explanation for their losses. Some people had chosen to travel another route. That was it. After the caravan disembarked the freight train in Guanajuato, half the group splintered and travelled north, hoping to enter through Texas. Mother had said the cartels were worse in that part of Mexico. Maybe they were the real monsters…

Rudy's belly rumbled as it had for the last week and he hoped his mother would come back soon.

He looked across the way and spotted Guillermo and his son Enrique. Guillermo's shirt appeared tighter on him as if he had gained weight over the last few days. Rudy wondered how the man had stayed so plump while everyone else starved. He was eating well and Rudy hated him for it. He hated Enrique too, for being gifted so nice a hat. Dark people like him were seldom given anything but mean stares.

Rudy's mom suddenly approached the camp. She smiled at him, placed two slabs of meat onto a pan, and set it down over the fire.

"I helped the owner of another butcher shop clean down his counters," she said. "I think I'm on to something."

The sizzle of the meat had stirred a few curious onlookers who soon returned to their starved slumber.

After dinner Rudy slept well and dreamt of the promise of a new country.

They'd crossed the Sonoran Desert and headed further north, where they now made camp in the Tijuana countryside, just outside a colony of concrete and sheet metal huts. There were just twenty people in the group. His mother had been right; people disappeared in this country left and right.

Rudy crouched alone beside the campfire where his mother had told him to wait. He dwelled on the border, now just a half day's walk away.

Guillermo buried his face into his hands and sobbed beside Rudy. Enrique had vanished as evening came and Rudy couldn't help but feel guilty. Maybe if they'd been friends, they could've watched over each other.

"My son is gone," Guillermo said. "Will no one help me find him?"

"You have nothing to cry about, you monster," shouted one of the women. "We know you've been snatching children in the night and slaughtering them to keep yourself fed."

"No, I, I don't know what you're talking about."

"That's right, said an old man. "We've been talking about it. Interesting how all of us are starving, yet you keep getting fatter. How do you explain that?"

The rest of the adults in the group stood and surrounded Guillermo. One of the men pulled on his collar. Rudy stood and stepped away. He hoped his mother would hurry back.

"No, wait, I can explain." Guillermo reached for his wallet. "Look," he said retrieving a wad of cash. "In Honduras, I was a wealthy man. I've been buying food."

"And you didn't think to share with us. When so many of us were starving?" The woman said.

The group hauled him off into the dark of the country until Rudy could no longer see them. Guillermo's screams faded after a while.

Rudy smiled as his mom returned from Tijuana. He'd never felt so relieved.

As always, she returned with two thin strips of meat. One for her and one for him. She slapped them on the pan over the fire and brought Rudy against her body.

"Tomorrow a new life begins for us," she said. She retrieved something from a small plastic bag. "I found you this hat, Mijo. I think you'll like it."

She secured a worn *Cruz Azul* hat on his head. It felt moist and warm.

Body of Work; or, The Fever Dreams of a Parasite

Ximena Mezcal, writing for *Divine Couture Magazine*

From his modest studio in Sierra Madre, California, the man adjusts his horn-rimmed glasses and pores over his laptop, meticulously looking over designs as his seamstress, Sylvia, puts the finishing touches on a dress for a client. The client: A snobby middle-aged housewife from Brentwood, he confides in me. He smirks, a playful, sarcastic crease that cuts across his face, a stark contrast to the frail and weathered visage of 73-year-old Mexican fashion icon, Alberto Madrigal.

Many will remember the maestro, who in the '80s and '90s, regularly shocked the industry with his outlandish designs and playful, gender-blurring fashion. Back when the sort of thing wasn't as in vogue as it is today. When only fashion-conscious mavericks dared to parade his whimsical men's line of charro-inspired suits, sharply tailored vests, and enormous sequined sombreros. The women's line equally as iconic; its vibrant, floral dresses strapped with bandoliers inspired by revolutionary troops and the folkish La Catrina of Madrigal's native Mexico.

His label, Madrigal, which carries his namesake, is still in business today, though they've since shifted focus to women's wear almost exclusively. Before I ask him why that is, Sylvia receives a call. She leans into Madrigal's ear and he nods sympathetically. She grabs her things and darts away. Madrigal tells me her son has become ill and needs to be picked up from school. He smiles, a weary gaze painting his face, the heavy bags drooping under his eyes hinting of countless sleepless nights.

Madrigal takes over the garment Sylvia was working on. He mentions that he offered her a job when she was a young, homeless immigrant, scared, alone, and new to this country. She helped him sew his dresses and has stayed on ever since. Twelve years now. She has repaid his kindness with unflinching loyalty, having stuck it out with him through thick and thin. Even through his depressive episodes throughout the last decade, a timespan which found Madrigal reclusive and shying away from the public eye. Which is why I have sought him out and set up this interview.

As he takes a pair of shears across a sheet of lilac silk, I ask him why he's seemingly abandoned the industry that so loved him. Why he's stopped designing for the hottest models and A-list actors? He shakes his head and begins to jab pins into the floral dress draped over the mannequin. It is a flowing, ethereal piece that will undoubtedly make its future owner very happy. Madrigal shifts focus and talks about his looming mortality, his legacy; how he never had children. I look around. A half-dozen mannequins loiter in the shadowed nooks near the back of the studio, their limbless torsos facing him as if hanging on his every word. They are unsettling. They are his only children, he jokes, as he follows my gaze. He glances over the framed magazine covers decorating the wall behind his desk. They bear the likeness of exotic supermodels wearing his most iconic garments. He's not pleased with his body of work, he says; he wants to leave a lasting impression on the world. Yes, he knows he's had a successful career. And that his endeavors have offered him a comfortable life. Yet, everything that came before is not enough. He feels the urge to do something that's never been done or seen before in an industry that constantly regurgitates terrible ideas. His words. Don't get him started on AI and the way brands have begun to incorporate its soulless designs into their fashion, removing the human element altogether.

How has Madrigal's label survived? Lately, Madrigal's clients have consisted of wealthy single mothers from Beverly Hills or porn stars looking for dresses to wear to the AVAs. But that's coming to an end, he says. He stares off into the distance, a pained look on his face. He needs to create something no one will ever forget. He's just not certain what that is yet.

As he drones on about his perceived failures, he yips as he pricks himself on a pin. Blood seeps out from his index finger and drips onto the fabric splayed out on the table. He sucks on his finger. I ask if he's alright. The pain, he says, is so insignificant to the pain of being unfulfilled. It is a deep chasm of the soul. "An emptiness so profound that it borders on suffering." Pure poetry. He steps back, disregards the dress, and admires the mannequin with all those pins sticking out of it. A human pincushion, he remarks. Sometimes, he says, he feels the same. I sense in him the ramblings of a tormented man at the end of his thread.

Either by a stroke of luck or divine intervention, there comes a knock outside the studio door. Heavy metal star Kane Krieger, a six-foot-five, boot-wearing, leather-clad, long-bearded monstrosity of a man, shuffles nervously inside. It's quite a sight. But at Madrigal's studio, you never know who will walk through those doors.

Madrigal and Krieger shake hands and exchange brief pleasantries. The stalwart Krieger dwarfs the five-foot Madrigal, who tilts his head back just to capture the enormity of the man before him.

The skinny: It just so happens that the premiere of Krieger's directorial debut horror film, *Fever Dreams of a Parasite,* is set to screen in a few weeks. The plot revolves around a man tormented by dreams which may be messages coming from some otherworldly place and his slow descent into madness.

Madrigal shares an anecdote about when he first arrived to the States when he'd been called a parasite and accused of leeching off people's taxes, stealing jobs from American fashion designers. He'd face taunts and insults from fellow dressmakers urging him to go back to Mexico City to sew dresses for burros. Krieger frowns and nods, an empathetic look on his face. Or his best imitation of one. Krieger says he doesn't know about all that but he admires Madrigal and always has, ever since he'd tailored a dress for his ex-wife, porn star Laura Banks, a couple years back. He asks, nay pleads Madrigal for a custom piece. Something unique, something that will make a splash at his premiere. Critics have panned his movie as worthless schlock at advanced screenings. He wants to shock the world. A big "Fuck You" to shove in the critics' faces.

Madrigal rubs his chin. He says he's never done something like this. For someone like Krieger. After a moment of contemplation, he beams. I know the look of realization well. Some little lightbulb has gone off over his head. Madrigal nods and says he's the parasite for him. Madrigal quickly takes Krieger's measurements and sends him off. His clients, he tells me, are delicate flowers like himself; thin, self-centered with fragile egos that wilt at the first insult or negative critique. But Krieger is different—doesn't care what anyone thinks. His kind of person. As he watches the giant leave his studio, he says wishes he had thick skin like Krieger's.

But a different look has come over Madrigal now. His brown eyes gleam with fire. Embers stoked with renewed vigor.

It appeared destiny had come calling. A gift dropped on Madrigal's lap. I ask him for a follow-up interview. Just to check in and see if his work with Krieger bears any fruit. He nods. But nothing would prepare me, or the world, for what came next.

Two weeks later I would get a call from Madrigal in the middle of the night, his voice low, his breaths short and labored.

Madrigal doesn't give me much time to get a word in before rambling about his failed attempts at designing Krieger's suit, his frustrations, his wastebasket overflowing with crumpled sketches. He's labored for days, he says, obsessing over something that thematically screams *parasite*. But nothing comes. Then, he tells me how his manic state has left him creatively spent and physically exhausted. That very night, after a laborious design session, he'd slumped into his chair and nodded off. Then came the details about the dream that followed.

He describes the dream as staccato bursts of vivid imagery. Strange, incohesive little visions, like morse code, messages, he feels, from some Great Beyond. A shadowed realm born in the mind, he surmises. Not quite Heaven, not quite Hell, but something different altogether. Most of what he says doesn't make sense. I'm tired and groggy and listening to the ramblings of a madman.

In the dream, he rambles, he'd wandered naked through a dark void, a sea of stars twinkling fervently above. Like fireflies. Horrendous-looking insects, not of this world, he claims, erupted from patches of muddy earth and latched onto his naked skin, driving their pincers and proboscis into his limbs, suckling on his essence. Eventually, they sucked him dry, leaving only a husk of his former self. A rind of skin that still had a vague semblance of the man he'd been in his previous life. His sagging face, every unique mole and birthmark still etched on his skin. He was woken by his dog who had been nipping at his fingers. Spotting something curious, Madrigal bent over, finding fleas crawling along the dog's spine. That's when an idea comes to him. *Parasites.*

He tells me he's cancelling the rest of our interview. That he has work to do and that I should attend Krieger's premiere. That I'd be witness to something truly beautiful. He hangs up. I don't go back to sleep.

Hollywood Boulevard. The historic Egyptian Theater. Site of the first Hollywood movie premiere in 1922. I wonder how Krieger managed to book this place as I stand in the open-air courtyard, ambling behind the cordoned velvet ropes separating the press from the red carpet. Photographers fidget on their phones. It's just another B-movie premiere, more pictures for their articles, blogs, clickbait fluff pieces.

One by one, the film's stars arrive, parading up the red carpet in their finest tuxedos and glamorous dresses, smiling for the press until they fade past the giant columns by the entrance.

It's been two weeks since my last contact with Madrigal. Subsequent calls prove unsuccessful. On a return trip to his studio, I find the business closed. As the days roll on, mild inquisitiveness leads to full-blown curiosity and sleepless nights. What could have possibly happened? Could this project have been the reinvigorating spark he'd so dreamed? Had it consumed him?

A black stretch limo pulls up to the curb. Krieger steps out onto the red carpet and the crowd lets out a collective gasp. People shove and rush toward the front of the street. I elbow and slip my way past the throng of reporters, jockeying for position amongst the rabid onlookers. A crowd has gathered around Krieger. Pedestrians, fans, the press.

Krieger is garbed in a purple vest, black slacks, and fine leather shoes. But there's something else. When I see it, I feel my mouth drop, my jaw goes slack, and the hairs on my neck go prickly. Madrigal, the old tailor, is draped over Kane Krieger's back, adorning his massive shoulders like fur. Only it's not Madrigal. Not anymore. His skin is flattened, stretched, splayed, and stitched onto Krieger's purple leather vest like a shawl or cape. Like a parasite. A tick latched onto a dog's spine. Madrigal's rubbery arms wrap around the rockstar's neck in a soft embrace as his pale legs fall around Krieger's waist, his small feet sewn onto the hem of the vest. Alberto Madrigal's flat head falls over Krieger's right shoulder, bobbing up and down with every step up the red carpet. His eyes are dark, hollow cavities gazing into space.

Flashes go off like twinkling stars, like fireflies, and for a moment I swear I see a hollowed-out smile etched on Madrigal's lifeless face.

Madrigal, as made apparent by the gasps and shrieks, achieves what he'd set out to do. A ghastly masterpiece, a fitting bookend to an incredible body of work that will certainly leave people talking for years. Flesh as fashion.

I pray it doesn't become a new trend.

After the premiere, Krieger is arrested for his part in the macabre stunt and faces felony charges for desecrating the dead. His film becomes a smash box office hit, a morbid sensation around the world.

Subsequent calls to Sylvia go unanswered. That very day, her son is pulled inexplicably from school and her phone number becomes deactivated. Her whereabouts are still unknown. The corpse, as of this writing, is still missing.

The Madrigal clothing line, despite its abrupt end, becomes something of a collector's item. A hot resale commodity on eBay and auction blocks with used garments fetching ungodly sums of money. As for Madrigal. I only hope he's found peace and happiness at last in that Great Beyond.

Effigies of Monstrous Things

His world shook and the earth opened like a maw to swallow him and Julia whole, their bodies tumbling down a muddy, chthonic pit where the shadows slithered like eels. The sensation of falling is what jostled him awake. Instinctively, he reached for Julia and grabbed a handful of the comforter where his wife should have been.

The back of his head was damp, as was the pillow cradling it. Marissa stood in front of the window, a beam of waning sunlight creating an orange halo around her as she rocked his shoulder with gentle hands.

"Papi, it's happening again," his five-year-old said in a soft voice. "And the air conditioner is broken, too."

The sun sank below the window and Mario grunted as his eyes adjusted to the growing darkness. The air conditioner sputtered as it blew warm, suffocating air through rusted vents. The smell of mildew wafted across the room, the source of which he couldn't identify. He sat up. In the heat and all that sweat his shirt had stuck to his body like a second skin. "I'll look into it, baby."

Satisfied with his answer, she skipped out of the room, her curly brown locks bouncing with every hop. His lungs burned and his throat felt raw again, as if he'd swallowed a handful of jagged rocks.

Mario shook off the discomfort and lifted the frame he kept on the nightstand. In the picture, Julia beamed, her amber eyes glistening with what joy remained at that point in their marriage. Marissa had inherited her mother's brown, curly hair. The hair of a goddess he used to say. Julia hadn't crossed his mind in ages. How long had it been since she'd left? He walked to the bathroom as he plumbed the depths of his mind, but it was all a haze—The answer wouldn't come. He shook his head. His memories lately had been filled with holes, like a cotton t-shirt decimated by moths.

The dreams, though, had become frequent. Nonsensical terrors. Visions wherein his family met strange, horrible fates he'd rather not dwell upon. He chalked it up to the pressures of being a single parent while working the lumber yard and attending night school for a nursing degree. Which reminded him…

A quick glance at the clock on the wall confirmed his fear: he was running late. He shuffled into the shower and turned on the water, waiting for it to run hot. The pipes groaned behind the walls. As the steam billowed, he pursed his lips. The showerhead was speckled with scum and black mold, as were the grooves between the tile walls. Not again. He could've sworn he'd scrubbed it clean. Mario soaked a cloth with bleach and wiped down the walls and the showerhead.

After a quick shower he opened his sock drawer and stared at the empty orange pill bottle. Fuck. It looked like he'd have to get by on will power tonight. He got dressed and padded into the kitchen. Marissa and Yvette were at the dining table hunched over their homework. Something was missing. He regarded the old booster chair tucked behind the table that had grown dusty. Why hadn't he ever thrown it away? Nostalgia, perhaps. Memories trying their damndest to cling on to what little life they had left.

"Where's your sister?" Mario asked no one in particular.

Yvette sipped from a glass of water, eyed him quizzically, and returned her attention to her schoolwork.

"It's just us two, Papi," Marissa said, gripping a red crayon as she scribbled on a sheet of paper. She'd sketched some abstract monster with horns, a large tail, and a multitude of small, crab-like pincers running the length of its torso.

"What are you guys working on?"

"Finishing up my book report on Charlotte's Web," Yvette said, her eyes fixed on her paper. She was studious, certainly more so than he'd ever been at ten.

"We're supposed to draw something for Halloween," Marissa said, "a monster of our own making." She stood and pinned her drawing on the fridge with a magnet.

"Aren't they all?" Mario said.

"Sink's leaking again," Yvette said, coughing into her hand. She cleared her throat. "Mr. Hartwell cut corners. Like always."

Mario grabbed a small flashlight from the junk drawer and crouched by the cabinet under the sink. He opened the doors and tossed the light around until he spotted the spring in the PVC pipe. Gray water wept from the elbow joint in a steady trickle, pooling directly underneath.

"Shit," he muttered, quickly lifting his shirt over his nose. Black mold had taken hold along the drywall backing. Mario lowered the shirt from his face and backed away from the sink. He fetched a pot, slid it under the leaky pipe, and closed the doors. "I'll talk to Mr. Hartwell tomorrow. Just stay clear of the cabinet. And don't drink from the tap."

"He's not going to do anything." Yvette pushed her glass away with two fingers.

"I'll be extra persuasive. Anyway, I gotta get to class. You know the routine."

"Be in bed by nine at the latest," Marissa said.

"That's right, baby," Mario said, smiling. "Love you, girls. I'll be back later."

A wave of humidity enveloped him as soon as he stepped outside. Beads of moisture began to dot his brow. It was early autumn but in Los Angeles, summer still had its say. He locked the door and when he turned, he noticed Miss Lucinda in her wheelchair, the tank of oxygen at her side. She peered blankly out over the second-floor guard rail which overlooked the courtyard of the apartment complex.

Her son, Marvin, was a substance abuser who'd vanished some time ago, devoured by the city like so many others. The man never got the help he needed. Not from his friends, not from the city, no one. And Miss Lucinda was too old to do anything about it. She'd been hindered by her COPD and other financial hardships. Just like everyone here.

"Good evening, Miss Lucinda," Mario said. She said nothing as she turned her attention across the street. These days, she didn't say much of anything.

Mario followed Miss Lucinda's gaze towards a neglected billboard looming over the neighborhood liquor store. The corner flap of a faded movie poster had peeled away, revealing the graffiti painted on the backboard. It was a red, snaking pinwheel that terminated in what appeared to be a horned head on one end. The billboard's LED underlighting created an eerie, hellish effect on the enigmatic image.

Mario made his way downstairs, his hand catching rusty flakes as he clutched the rail. He wiped his palm on his scrubs. Everything in this complex was falling apart.

At the gate, he checked his mailbox and rifled through the day's correspondence. Nothing but a stack of bills. Most days he felt his debt was insurmountable. A malady he'd carry to the grave. Even subsidized housing couldn't unburden him.

When he got to the bottom of the stack, he saw another one of those Have You Seen Me? cards with the picture of a missing child. This one he thought he'd spotted playing in the neighborhood not too long ago. Jackie Hodges. A Black boy. Twelve. Last week it had been a little Latina girl, but her name eluded him. She'd had brown skin, an infectious smile, and wild, curly hair like Marissa's. Disappearances had become too frequent a thing around this part of town. He wondered if everyone just crumpled up the cards, moved on and forgot about them. The thought of his own children disappearing caused a flutter in his stomach. Like a monster lurking over his shoulder.

There was nothing more he wanted than to pack up and leave. Anywhere but the inner city. But he lacked the means—the money. Mario peered up at his apartment, thinking about his girls. They deserved so much more. He contemplated the barred windows, the metal screen doors, the great wrought iron fence barricading the perimeter of the complex. Never in his life had he felt so much like a prisoner.

Every day it felt like the world was conspiring against him and people that looked like him—subtle cruelties that kept him down. Thousands of small cuts that amounted to slow exsanguination.

Unquantifiable little crimes.

They could tell you exactly how many people had been murdered in L.A. County last year, but they could never tell you how many times a colored man got turned down at the bank for a loan, or lost out on a job offer for speaking a certain way. Phantom infractions that could ruin a life and keep someone locked up in a place like this.

Before he walked out the gate, Mario spotted Hartwell in the courtyard smoking a cigarette beneath a sky the color of bruised flesh. Hartwell's eyes followed a young boy riding his bike on the curb as the street lights flickered on.

"Evening, Jake," Mario said.

Hartwell turned his face away and blew out a cloud of smoke, hacking as he did. His mustache had bristled with yellow, nicotine-stained hairs. He wore his typical jeans, boots, and a white shirt spattered with red paint. He'd more than likely been tending to one of his better properties in the suburbs. "Hey, Mario. What's the word, amigo?"

"Hey, listen, my pipes are leaking again, the air conditioner's busted, and I've got mold growing all over the place. Can you help a brother out?"

"Yeah, I'll get to it," he said with disinterest in his voice. Hartwell took a hearty drag from his cigarette and turned away.

"I've got two girls in there, Jake. I don't want them breathing in that mold. Can you handle the leaks at least? Maybe replace those old pipes?"

Smoke flared out his nostrils. "Mhm."

"Listen, Jake, we both know I'm within my right to report you. You've left us hanging too many times. The whole fucking place is falling apart."

Hartwell dropped his cigarette and stomped it out. "You do that and I'll call Child Services on your ass. They won't like that my tenant is a meth addict who leaves his girls home alone at night."

Mario gritted his teeth and balled his fists. "You know I have night school, Jake. It's fucking hard enough as it is on a single father."

"Like I said, amigo, I'll get to it." Hartwell grinned and walked towards his van.

Subtle cruelties. Unquantifiable crimes.

Mario's fists unclenched. He was used to feeling powerless, but the thought of his girls getting sick didn't sit with him. He had to do something. And it wasn't just him. It was common knowledge that the other tenants had been dealing with the leaky faucets and sinks, dirty water, broken air conditioners, and that persistent mold no one could seem to expunge. The heat and moisture had no doubt spread the rot, circulating it through the vents. It seemed like it'd been going on forever.

The flashlight, he realized, had been in his pocket. Perhaps he could look for himself. He wasn't an expert, but maybe it had something to do with the aging plumbing system. Fuck, it was worth a shot.

Mario shoved the mail back in the box and made his way around the back of the building where the boiler room was located. Overgrown weeds were there to greet him in an empty lot where bedsheets fluttered from clotheslines like ghosts. He tried the door to the boiler room but it was locked. Of course.

Moonlight caught on heaps of dirt that had been piled along the lot as if there had been some recent excavation. What appeared to be wheelbarrow tracks cut across the lot and led to an old grate on the bottom of the wall. There was a chance he could find access to the boiler room from there.

After looking around to make sure no one had seen him, he pried the cover loose, crouched inside, and waved his light around. The crawlspace was tight, just big enough for him to duckwalk through. As he squatted past the mouth of the crawlspace, his socks and shoes sopped up moisture from the muddy ground. Once inside, a wave of oppressive heat swarmed his body and it wasn't long before sweat began to trickle down his face and seep into his eyes.

Ducking below the joists, Mario followed a maze of corroded copper pipes which dribbled from their joints. Everywhere he looked, black-blue fuzz covered the rotten beams above. The building moaned as it settled, specks and spores fell from the planks and danced in the cone of his light. Mario sneezed into the crook of his arm. A subtle tingling sensation filled his nose and ran down his throat.

The crawlspace terminated abruptly where a plywood wall bisected the building. The pipes descended into a small cavity—a six-foot plunge into a concrete floor that stretched into darkness. The pitter-patter of droplets echoed in the distance. He considered turning back but he'd already be marked as absent from class tonight. May as well keep going. He sighed and wriggled down the hole which was just big enough for him to slide through.

At the bottom, he found himself inside a narrow tunnel, the walls carved from the earth itself as if the place had been hastily buried and bored through again. Rows of large, dusty iceboxes had been stacked on the floor along the walls. Old Igloo coolers; the kind you took to the beach in the summer.

Mario wrinkled his nose. The air smelled of decay. Like spoiled meat and mildew. He followed the pipes on the ceiling until the tunnel opened to a dim, spacious room filled with old water heaters, broken pumps, rusted pipes, and assorted HVAC equipment. Above, a few overhead light fixtures swayed lazily to invisible currents of air. An antiquated boiler room. Subterranean remnants from an older Los Angeles.

The building groaned again, this time like a wounded animal, and earth sifted from the ancient walls. He heard the drip of water. His light skimmed past something glimmering, moving with inky fluidity. A fountain. A bird bath, really, overflowing with murky water. It had been placed directly beneath a leak springing from the ceiling.

Behind the fountain his light caught the outline of something peculiar. As he approached, his probing light touched the jagged thing and it cast a shadow against the wall, imbuing it with the illusion of life. The thing in question appeared to be a sculpture of a horrendous winged demon, its serpentine form a depiction of tanned flesh and exposed bone. Like an excavated fossil or mummified beast. It stood on a round, raised platform of marble. Mario ogled it, partly in fear, but also in bewilderment. Who had made this? The thing looked like it had been crafted from plaster and PVC pipe matted with papier mâché, but upon closer inspection it reeked of rot. The longer he gazed upon it the more he had the suspicion the abhorrent thing had been a patchwork of leathery skin grafted onto human bones.

Mario stepped toward the sculpture. His heart raced. If his nursing studies had done anything, they had confirmed that his suspicions were true. What stood before him was a jigsaw of disparate anatomy. A human pelvic bone formed the base of its head, where coccyges jutted from either side of the crest like makeshift horns. The obturator foramen appeared like gaping eyes, black holes staring back at him, judging him.

A mandible had been fused to the bottom of the pubic bone, its teeth removed and replaced with a row of severed pinkies. An abnormally long spine ran down its head forming a faux serpentine tail that stretched deep into the shadowed recesses of the boiler room, fused, he surmised from multiple human vertebrae. Several ribcages had been joined to cover the length of its spine. Outstretched humerus bones and fanned-out fingers extended from its back, webbed with taut skin like bat wings.

The demon sculpture bore femurs and tibias for arms with elongated fingers for hands, made from numerous proximal bones. Rows of small, crab-like claws sprouted from its ribs. They appeared to be small human hands, their digits removed, except for the thumb and forefinger to give the appearance of clawed appendages.

Mario stepped back, a rush of bile surging up his throat. What had he stumbled onto? He approached one of the iceboxes along the wall and flipped the lid. The rotting remains of children, all packed tightly in various states of decay, greeted him. Hips, hands, faces, scalps bearing curly, brown hair. Putrid flesh mingling with bone shards. One bore a face resembling that little boy, Jackie Hodges.

He opened another. It held only bones, like an ossuary. This couldn't be real. He moved on to another cooler and opened the lid. Julia stared back with lifeless eyes, her cheeks sunken in, her skin swathed in blue-gray mold. Her head sat atop a pile of discarded organs and fatty tissue. The rest of her was gone.

A wave of nausea overcame him and his breaths became shallow, burning gasps. He stumbled over his feet. The world began to spin and blur. Footfalls echoed down the tunnel, a muffled voice following close behind. He turned off the flashlight and threw himself behind a water pump just as Hartwell entered the boiler room.

Mario made himself small and peered from behind the pump. His landlord stepped towards the fountain, cupped his hands inside, and brought the water to his lips, drinking like a man deprived. Hartwell muttered to himself in hushed tones, stringing together crazed sentences Mario could just barely make out.

"It slumbers beneath…shall awaken once more…blessed be this effigy, born in tribute to its splendor."

Mario pressed his back to the pump and felt warm tears stream down his face. All those children. Julia. But she'd left him ages ago, hadn't she? The way she looked, she couldn't have been dead that long.

"The sculpture is nigh complete…just a few more bones…a few more *children*."

His mind reeled as he thought about his girls. He needed to get back to them. Call the police. Mario's lungs suddenly began to burn. A tingle ran up his nose. He cupped his hands over his face and fought the urge to cough, to sneeze, to yell and cry.

In the depths of the boiler room, he thought he saw movement, as if the shadows themselves were dancing, slithering, coiling into themselves.

The building creaked as its old bones settled. Spores fell from the ceiling, dusting his world like snowfall. The fire in his lungs spread to his throat. His eyes watered and stung and itched. He sneezed.

Hartwell emerged from behind the pump, his body appeared to be covered in a black aura, a seething energy of shadowy, writhing tendrils. Mario felt himself lifted off the ground and dragged to the fountain.

"Drink," said Hartwell.

Mario felt his limbs grow weak, his consciousness slipping. What was happening?

"Drink!"

Mario's face splashed into the cool water and felt it slither up his nose, down his throat. A rancid taste filled his mouth and singed his tongue.

There came a voice from nowhere and everywhere at once.

"Make me whole again."

Mario tried to scream for help but no words came. His throat became coarse, a useless meat pipe. All around, the spores fell, clinging to his clothes, his skin, his lungs.

The voice came again.

"Make me whole. Finish the effigy."

And then, darkness.

Mario woke in his bed, damp, covered in sweat. The dreams had spiraled into haunting, turbulent affairs. How long had they been going on now?

The air conditioner sputtered as it exhaled hot air, spreading the smell of mildew. The sun sank beneath his window and the world grew dark. He cursed under his breath. Time to get ready.

As he sat up, Julia eyed him with loving eyes from the frame at his bedside. A familiar pang festered in the pit of his stomach. How long had it been since she'd left him? The answer wouldn't come. All he knew was that he still missed her.

In the bathroom, the walls of the shower were covered in mold. He thought he'd cleaned it. It had become a tedious, laborious cycle. He'd make sure to speak to Hartwell. Running late, he ignored it and showered.

It wasn't until he got dressed that he noticed the house had been strangely quiet.

He walked into the kitchen. Yvette sat at the dining table hunched over a book. She sipped from a glass of water, looked at him, and returned to her reading.

"Where's your sister?" he asked, looking around the kitchen. It felt spacious, empty.

Yvette looked up from her paper, mildly irritated. "It's just me, dad."

"Right. Right."

He looked at the booster chair behind the table for a moment before his eyes settled on a sheet of paper pinned on the fridge. A juvenile crayon sketch of a terrible horned monster. He had no idea where it had come from. It seemed familiar and yet so alien. Like a memory stolen. Mario hung his head and wondered what other things he'd lose the next time he woke.

The Body Booth

"Now," Francis said, holding up a hand, "are you sure you're ready to see this? It's pretty sick shit."

Yazmina Mejia scowled. On more than one occasion she'd had to remind her editor that as a journalist in Ciudad Juárez, she'd seen every grotesquery one could imagine; cartel beheading videos, corpses dangling from freeway overpasses, scores of mutilated women pulled up from shallow graves. But that was a different life in a different place.

"You already know I can handle it," she said, adjusting her body as she sat in the chair across his desk. The furniture wasn't made to accommodate a pregnant woman. Not this late into a pregnancy, anyway.

Francis nodded, tapped the screen, and slid his phone across the desk. The candid video, which Yazmina presumed was recorded on a cheap burner phone, began with a pixelated low-angle shot of about a dozen men in tuxedos, their faces hidden by three-holed balaclavas. They sipped martinis and murmured amongst themselves in hushed tones. A few looked at something offscreen and gasped, their exposed mouths contorted in shock. The shot panned upward to reveal them crowding what appeared to be an old phone booth lit by a pair of overhead ceiling lamps.

The camera spun around a dim studio, its high ceiling, polished hardwood floors, and accented end tables adorned with extravagant vases, spoke to wealth and privilege. Whoever was recording suddenly squeezed past the crowd and approached the phone booth, their breaths increasingly short and labored. The shot stopped just a few paces shy of the booth.

Yazmina brought the knuckle of her index finger to her mouth and bit down. She couldn't be sure due to the low resolution, but what appeared to be a stretched epidermis pressed against the surface of the double glass doors; like someone shoving a pale belly against a window.

Yazmina looked at Francis. "What the fuck is that?"

Francis planted his elbows on the desk and steepled his fingers. "Keep watching."

Yazmina looked back down at the phone. The camera's operator had already entered the booth, shutting the doors behind themselves. The dim blue light of the booth's overhead bulb exposed its ghastly, encapsulated innards. She wasn't sure what she was seeing was real. How could it be? A canvas of pink connective tissue lined the ceiling and every pane of glass, throbbing to the tempo of a heartbeat. The camera approached the side of the booth where Yazmina could now make out thin purple blood vessels snaking along its walls. The flesh had a slick, wet sheen, like the insides of someone's stomach.

A hand stretched into the frame, flashed a scalpel, then disappeared from view. There came a deep grunt followed by the pinging of metal hitting the floor. The phone shifted between hands before a bloodied palm pressed against the wall of meat. Like little tongues, hundreds of fine hairs wriggled from porous crypts in the flesh-wall and lapped up its scarlet offering.

Yazmina winced and slid the phone back across the table before covering her mouth with one hand and cupping her belly with the other. "Is this some sick joke? Who sent this to you?"

"Anonymous text."

"Is it real?"

"Don't know. I want you to look into it."

Yazmina wasn't sure if Francis was pulling her leg. The paper had gotten its share of pranks and incredulous tips from time to time. In any case, if the video had been legitimate, this was something out of her league. "I'm an art columnist, Francis. Don't handle the gross stuff anymore."

"That's the thing," he said, smirking. "Whoever sent me that video claims this is part of some secret high society art exhibit."

Yazmina cleared her throat. "Come again?"

"Apparently that beauty there belongs to a Doctor Andrzej Severin. He calls it the Body Booth and hosts exclusive viewings for his closest friends." Francis scribbled something on a notepad, tore off a slip, and handed it to her. "I did some digging. He's a retired doctor. Regenerative medicine. He lives in a loft downtown. I need you to go and see what this is all about. And don't worry, the squirmy stuff is probably just practical effects, repurposed animatronics, what have you. But let's see what his angle is."

"And if it's real?" Yazmina didn't know why she'd asked. Of course, it wasn't real. It was all probably just some twisted idea of a prank. Some gag the creator of that video wanted going viral. Fake or not, the thought of that squirming mass of flesh had repulsed her in ways that desecrated bodies hadn't.

Francis' lips curled up devilishly, his eyes like flickering embers. "Then this newspaper will have quite a delectable story." He held up his hands as if framing a headline. "'World's most grotesque art exhibit.'"

Yazmina put the slip in her bag and excused herself. She didn't like the headline, the way his eyes lit up, the way his lips had curled into a hungry leer. Between that and the Body Booth, she wasn't sure which had upset her more.

A relic from the 1930s, it was an Art Deco Highrise just off Skid Row. Its faded, chipped facade standing shoulder-to-shoulder against the grimy walls of a cheap hotel and a shuttered appliance store under whose awnings squatters had taken refuge from the oppressive sun.

Yazmina let herself in through the front door. A rat skittered across the checkered floor of the grungy vestibule and out into the street. She cursed under her breath and pressed the buzzer corresponding to Severin's loft. While she waited, she pinched the bridge of her nose, massaging away the onset of a coming headache.

She quickly went over the notes she'd jotted down on the walk over from the car. Doctor Andrzej Severin was a thirty-year expert in regenerative medicine, specializing in in vitro grown organs and transplant surgery; topics she'd never touched in her career. Severin had been cited in countless studies she'd probably have to pore through later if the story checked out.

Yazmina groaned. What was she even doing here? The art column was temporary, she had to remind herself, at least until she worked her way up to something more meaningful. *The Times* had been a godsend, yes, and she was glad she wasn't working a dead-end local rag, but it was still a far cry from penning stories of corruption and political violence in a land that cultivated it widely. It was never an easy thing, starting all over in another country, especially at thirty-eight. At least here most people weren't trying to kill her for doing her job.

Just then her stomach rumbled as it began to cannibalize itself. The hunger pangs tugged sharply. She rubbed her belly, hoping it would be as much a comfort to Kiki as to herself. She regretted not grabbing breakfast and now lunch would have to wait, too.

"Who is it?" the speaker box on the wall squawked.

"Hello. My name is Yazmina Mejia. I'm an art columnist at *The Times*. I'm looking for a Doctor Andrzej Severin."

"What do you want?" the voice crackled in response.

Yazmina leaned into the box. "I was made aware of a certain art exhibit you host and I wanted to know if I could interview you."

"Leave and never return," the scrambled voice said.

Yazmina chortled. Spoken like a true curmudgeon or dime store horror novel spook. She thumbed the buzzer again, her lips almost touching the box. "I know about the Body Booth."

There came a long pause before the box crackled again. "Come inside," the voice said. The inner door of the vestibule buzzed. "I assume you already know where to find me."

Yazmina took the rickety lift to the topmost floor, took her time trudging down a narrow corridor, and hooked a left until she found the corresponding room. She rapped gently on his door. After a moment, she heard the deadbolts unlatch before the door creaked open.

On the other side of the doorway stood a lanky, geriatric man dressed in gray slacks and a brown wool vest. He stamped his walking cane on the hardwood floor, dragging his loafered feet as he crossed the threshold to greet her. It wasn't until he shuffled into the light of the hall that she saw his yellow eyes, the yellow tint of his skin. He extended a trembling jaundiced hand and a smile formed on his weathered face.

"Hello," the yellow man said, his voice gravelly, hoarse. "I am Doctor Andrzej Severin."

Yazmina smiled and shook his hand. His fingers were long and cold but surprisingly gentle.

"A pleasure to meet you, Doctor."

She lifted her gaze toward his wrist. It was as yellow as the rest of him and etched with scars. Some cuts looked fresh.

He locked onto her wandering eyes. "As you can see, I'm very ill. Please pay no attention to my malady." His eyes fell on her belly and his smile faded. "Expecting, I see. How far along now?"

"Eight months. This is Ki-"

"I never had children," he cut her off, pulling his hand away. "Never could make the time. Why don't you tell me what you want?"

"I'd like to ask about your exhibit, what it is, exactly. I'd like to know why you're hosting clandestine viewings for wealthy elites." She smiled again, hoping it would dull the bluntness of her probing.

His fingers curled around his cane like a spider. "I don't appreciate people coming to my door and making unwarranted claims."

Yazmina dug her phone from her back pocket and played the video for him.

When it finished, he scowled and nudged the door open. "I think," he said, grumbling, "it's time I begin culling my list of friends." He turned and shuffled back into the loft. "Maybe I'll ban phones next time."

Yazmina followed him inside a dim, spacious studio, its insides adorned with several abstract paintings, a few Greek busts, and a collection of expensive-looking Chinese vases alongside some potted ferns. Icy air pumped into the room, nicking at her skin like a torrent of needles. She wrapped her arms around her chest but it only partly mitigated the cold.

By the windows, motes of dust hung on a few slivers of sunlight piercing the parted scarlet drapes. Outside, the downtown Los Angeles skyline stared back.

Severin shut the door and fastened the deadbolt. Yazmina reached inside her bag and gripped the pepper spray she carried for situations like this.

The old man licked his cracked lips. "If you're going to write about it, I may as well show you." He waved a hand toward the installation. "So that there are no misconceptions."

She eased her hand off the pepper spray and followed his gaze. An old telephone booth sat under a pair of crossing overhead lamplights in the center of the room. Like the centerpiece of a museum exhibit.

"Have you ever given life to art?"

Yazmina nodded. "I've dabbled in some acrylic painting. Pastels, here and there. I minored in art history in college but journalism—"

Severin shook his head. "No, not created art; given life to it."

"I'm not sure I follow."

Severin sighed, jabbed his cane at the booth. "Well, this is what you came for, dear. Go on. Take a closer look."

She approached the booth timidly, unsure of it as if it were going to come alive, and…she didn't know what. Rip her apart? She was seeing it clearly now. Under the faded blue sign that read *Pacific Bell*, something repulsive pressed against the glass. Like in the video, there was a layer of flabby meat, its mass speckled with curly hair, pressing against the double glass doors from the inside, expanding and contracting as if it were taking shallow breaths. As far as she could tell there were no wires or cables running through the booth's frame, no pneumatic pumps giving the thing life.

A small white placard on one of the doors read:

Andrzej Severin, M.D.

American, 1950-

The Body Booth

Gastrointestinal Tissue on Telephone Booth

"Do you like my art piece?"

"I'm almost afraid to ask," Yazmina said, her eyes unable to break from the vulgar display of fat, skin, glass, and metal.

He placed his hand on a pane of glass. "The dermis of a belly. The inner portion is stomach lining tissue."

The hairs on the back of her neck stood erect. Yazmina turned to face him. She reached inside her bag and flicked on her digital voice recorder. "You're being serious. Did you cut up a few cadavers? Run a current through their flesh?"

Severin smirked. "Nothing so nefarious. Using a telephone booth as a scaffolding, I cultivated living tissue inside of it. Though, it's more an interactive art piece than something with a practical medical application."

"How exactly did you cultivate flesh?"

"I can't disclose that, dear. Several benefactors would like to maintain anonymity. I can tell you it involves DNA splicing, the use of hydrogels as cell carriers, things of that nature."

"You used the word *interactive*…"

He nodded. "Since the tissue walls have no digestive organs, their cells have been modified to ingest blood and its nutrients. Inside, you will find a scalpel lying on a table. Anyone is free to feed the Body Booth as they see fit. Or not."

She took two paces toward the booth. Any minute she expected Severin to cackle and tell her it was all a joke. That the art piece was nothing more than some elaborate prop meant to shock and disgust its audience. Just then the dermis squirmed, held in place firmly by the double glass doors. She swallowed back a lump of saliva. "What happens if no one chooses to feed it?"

"The tissue will rapidly degenerate and become necrotic. When not hosting an exhibit, I keep it alive through an intravenous blood drip connected through a port in the back of the booth. The drip is in turn hooked up to a small refrigeration unit."

"It? Alive?" She shook her head. "I'm sorry. I'm having a hard time believing any of this, Doctor."

"Oh, it's all very real. You're free to see for yourself." He tapped the cane against the doors.

"I mean...a sentient meat booth?" She placed her hand on the doors. "Even if this were all real, wouldn't that be a bit unethical? I doubt this is legal."

"It is something many people would find objectionable. Hence the secrecy, the selectiveness." Severin smiled. "Though, I have to correct you. The tissue is a functioning organism, yes, but it is not a sentient being. It has no brain to receive impulses that you and I would register as pain. Only mechanical stimuli. It is simply meat kept in a perpetually operating state. Any notion of a living thing is purely made manifest by the beholder's projection. The piece is meant to evoke empathy or guilt. To prove whether we are willing to let an organism perish or to keep it functioning when faced with the knowledge that we are its only source of sustenance, even though we know it not to be truly alive. Not in the way we typically perceive life, anyway."

She hadn't expected so much candor. It was almost too much to take in. "People really cut themselves to keep that thing alive?"

"A little pain for a little life. Donors can give as much as they'd like. Within reason of course. I closely monitor the bloodletting."

"Bloodletting." Yazmina repeated the word. Her palms became sweaty and she wiped them on the sides of her jeans. It all sounded like a fever dream. Living tissue growing inside a phone booth, blood drips, scalpels, bloodletting. It was all so... vampiric. She took a step backward. "I don't think I can do this." Pressure began to build up behind her eyes. Her head pounded terribly.

"No," Severin held up his hands. Pleading. "Please, look inside for yourself." He grabbed her wrist and led her toward the booth. He threw the double doors wide and they accordioned open to reveal walls of moist tissue throbbing inside. "Please, humor this old man."

She wanted to break free, to run for the door, but Severin had locked her inside. She exhaled. Best to oblige the old man. She'd known better than to incur a man's wrath, especially when locked alone in a room with him. When his animus waned, she'd make for the door, push the whole thing as far from her mind as possible. "Okay," she sighed. "I'll give it a look."

He smiled and released his grip. "Well, go on. Look for yourself."

Yazmina stepped inside the phone booth. Severin shut the doors behind her. Bolted on the panel in front of her was a vintage black phone propped on a shiny aluminum box. The kind you'd find littering every corner of the street thirty years ago; the same she had used in her youth to call her mother for a ride after school. Underneath the phone box was a small counter that used to hold those thick yellow phone books. Gone now was the phone book and in its place lay strewn several items. A scalpel, a bottle of rubbing alcohol, a bag of cotton swabs, some bandages. On either side of her shoulders, she heard the subtle, moist smacking sounds of something writhing. Hesitantly, she swiveled her head. Her insides twisted into knots at the sight of the panels, lined with wet, rosy tissue. The flesh had enveloped the ceiling as well. A whiff of funk slithered up her nostrils. Her mind recalled the image of a carved-out pumpkin, its stringy insides moist and musky.

The walls contracted and expanded gently, like a pair of healthy lungs. She didn't know why but she was overcome with an inexplicable urge to touch it. Yazmina raised a hand and brought it toward the flesh. Her index and middle fingers glided along one of the panels, tracing every smooth bump and valley of meat. The flesh felt soft, fatty, like the inside of her cheeks. Thick globs of mucus accumulated on her fingertips before fine strands of cilia-like hairs sprouted from tiny pores and bristled against her skin.

It was real. Tangible. Alive.

The air turned sour, like spoiled meat. Yazmina gagged and pivoted for the exit. Before she could throw the doors open, the flesh shriveled like a prune. The tissue's pink color began to fade to a grayish blue. Thin, snaking blood vessels contracted and turned a darker shade of purple. The booth became a necrotic organ of weeping blisters and open sores. Gastric ulcers seeped thin rivulets of blood and pus, the tributaries collecting into pools at her shoes, staining the rust-plated floor.

Yazmina reached for the scalpel, the blue overhead light glinting off its blade like shimmering stars. Wincing, she plucked it off the counter. There came a voice in her head, telling her to cut herself, to bleed.

Her head began to pound to the beat of her heart, which was now smashing against her chest like a piston. Yazmina bowled over with pain as she felt a sharp contraction. She dropped the scalpel and cradled her belly with one hand while she steadied herself on the counter with the other.

Brrriiinnngggg. The phone rang. The lining on the walls turned black as the blood vessels writhed like dying earthworms. A wave of nausea washed over her. Hot bile rushed up her throat, but she swallowed it back down. *Brrriiinnngggg*. The phone rang again. With a trembling hand, she unhooked the phone from the box. "Hungry," a crackling voice said. She slammed the phone on the cradle and stormed out of the booth.

Yazmina darted past Severin, glancing off his pleading hands. "You're fucking sick," she said as she unfastened the deadbolt. Without turning back, she fled the studio.

Yazmina kept a pregnancy diary. She wrote in it every night since she'd first learned she was going to be a mother. In it, she kept records of trivial things. Mundane things. But also things like detailed charts of her weight gain and the changes in her body.

But her favorite things were the little conversations she'd had with her daughter. Dialogues wherein Yazmina would ask Kiki how she had been feeling in the womb that particular day. Sometimes she would even write little poems for Kiki. The diary entries were something she could show her one day when she was old enough to understand what it all meant. How her mother had done the best she could all on her own, how she hadn't needed a man to see her through.

But for once this night, Yazmina didn't know what to write. Her pen kissed the ruled sheet of paper and lingered there, the ink bleeding into a little black splotch. How to explain to Kiki that she had witnessed a nightmare made manifest inside a box? A box of horrors. She considered how crazy the story would sound and decided to leave the page blank. One nightmare, at least, that would be spared on the mind of a child. Still, she wasn't so sure if what she'd seen was real herself. But it was. She had touched it. The oozing flesh. The bristling cilia. The rapidly decaying tissue.

Yazmina shut the diary.

What would she tell Francis? Maybe she'd chalk it up to nothing but a sick prank, hope he'd drop the whole thing. Then she could get on with writing about whatever new exhibit the Getty Museum was hosting. But she'd be lying to herself. What she saw *was* real.

The lid from the pot on the stove began to rattle as her soup boiled. Yazmina got up from the desk to silence its protests. On the way to the kitchen, she peered into the nursery. The crib sat there, half assembled, a dozen screws lain haphazardly on the floor. She made a note to finish it on the weekend. *If* she could wrap up her assignments before the deadline.

After dinner, Yazmina took her vitamins and plucked a picture book from her shelf. She'd made a routine of reading Kiki bedtime stories every night. Tonight, she'd gone with *The Very Hungry Caterpillar*. It was a childhood favorite of hers. How the voracious caterpillar had morphed into a beautiful butterfly was something she had taken to heart. The metamorphosis had spoken to her in profound ways, even at an early age. And change came in many ways. She'd gone through many in her own life. At puberty, when her own body had gone through changes, and she would be teased by the boys in class; when she had decided to switch majors and focus on journalism; deciding to leave her native country when the death threats were hitting close to home; ditching the man she thought she'd loved when the hands he'd placed on her ceased to be tender. Change was beautiful. The fact hadn't been lost on her now with the pregnancy.

It wasn't long before she'd settled into bed when her phone rang, its shrill chime startling her. She sat upright and plucked it off the nightstand.

The number was unlisted. Still, she answered.

"Hello?"

"Ms. Mejia," the coarse voice said. Severin.

"How the hell did you get my number?"

"You handed me your business card, don't you remember?"

"Maybe I'm in a bit of a fog but I don't remember doing so." She felt Kiki kick as the words left her mouth. The fetal movements had grown frequent at this stage in the pregnancy. She shut her eyes and took a deep breath. "Anyway, why are you calling?"

"Do you intend to complete your piece about me?"

"I'm not sure yet."

"If you do, all I ask is that you write honestly about what you experienced. But also, that you do so with grace. For the sake of this old man."

For a moment she sat there, silent. She'd been accused of many things in this life, but being a shit journalist was not one of them. Art column be damned, she would do this story right.

"I want to go through with it," she said. "I want to feed the booth. It's the only way I can write an honest piece. I'll decide for myself what's real."

"It's your decision, of course."

"I know. How about tomorrow afternoon? Say, three?"

"Yes. That's fine."

"By the way," she said, before hanging up. "I wasn't amused when you called me inside the booth and said you were hungry."

"Ms. Mejia," Severin said. "The phone is not connected."

Francis didn't show up at work the next morning. It was just as well. Once she had settled into her desk, Yazmina transcribed everything she'd taped on the voice recorder onto her notebook. Most of it was muffled gibberish. Severin had mentioned using the phone booth as a scaffolding. She wondered if there was any significance to using an old phone booth. Or was it just the hip thing to do? A modern art piece juxtaposing antiquated technology with revolutionary science? Maybe it just fit a practical need.

She fast-forwarded to the end of their meeting. Just after he'd grabbed her and told her to step inside and look for herself. Nothing but static. She pressed her ear to the recorder, hoping to hear the ringing of the phone but there was only the crackling of the device shifting around inside her bag.

After work, she drove back to Severin's studio. He opened the door and flashed a crooked smile. Even his teeth were yellow. "I'm glad you changed your mind."

"Let's get it over with." She reached into her bag and thumbed the recorder on.

Severin nodded. "I'm going to disconnect the blood drip," he said. "Enter at your convenience." The doctor hobbled toward the back of the booth and vanished from view.

Yazmina pulled the double dermal doors open. Inside, the blue overhead light, which the flesh had grown around, hinted at the shifting of meat. She stepped into that confined space and shut the doors.

It was as she remembered it. An encapsulated box of squirming, throbbing tissue. A living organ growing inside a phone booth. A blasphemous work of art.

She ran her hand along one of its fleshy walls. The hairs—the cilia—bristled against her fingers, almost playfully. Like feelers exploring something new and alien. The wall suddenly retracted and grew taut as it began to lose color. The blood vessels writhed and shriveled.

Yazmina felt her heart sink into her stomach. It was an awful feeling watching a thing die in front of you, suffering. Sucking in a deep breath, she reached for the scalpel on the counter. She gritted her teeth as she sliced diagonally along her left hand; a one-inch incision across the meaty part of her palm. Slowly, she brought her hand up to the wall. Blood dripped down her wrist as she hesitated and left her hand lingering in the space between them.

What was she doing?

She exhaled and pressed her hand to the wall. The cilia brushed against her skin with fervor, prickling her, probing her gash like minuscule tongues. In seconds the fine hairs had lapped up every drop of blood.

It wasn't enough. Somehow, she knew. She again brought the scalpel to her hand, wincing as the tip punctured her flesh and slid across her palm, opening the gash another inch. Setting the blade on the counter, she took her right thumb and index finger and pinched, drawing as much blood from the wound as she could. She pressed her palm to the wall and again the cilia bristled her skin, exploring the slit on her hand like a ravenous creature.

It hadn't been thirty seconds before the tissue began to regain its pinkish color. Engorged on their meal, the blood vessels swelled and throbbed with what she assumed was satisfaction.

"There you go," she said. "All better."

Life. She had given the thing life. Or at least kept it alive. As she dabbed her palm with cotton swabs, Yazmina couldn't help but smile. It was a thing of wonder.

Later, after nearly everyone had emptied out for the night, she returned to her office, fired up the desktop, and fanned out a few manila folders over the desk. She ran her bandaged hand through her hair and sighed. "Okay," she said under her breath, "let's see what we can dig up."

She pored over documents, medical journals, and news articles; everything she could find on Doctor Andrzej Severin.

The first item was a short biography from a St. Joseph's Hospital website, where Severin had previously held a residency. According to it, Severin's mother, Anita, was diagnosed with coronary artery disease and passed away forty years ago after failing to procure a heart transplant. Since that time, he had become a respected doctor and surgeon, dedicating his life to regenerative medicine, artificial organs, novel stem cell research, and experimental procedures.

He had mentioned hydrogels. Yazmina made note to dig further into that.

There were a few public records about his philanthropy. He'd donated to cancer research programs and universities. He was also apparently an avid art collector. A couple of papers had run stories about Severin's more notable acquisitions through some big auctions.

Her phone vibrated. An email from Francis. He was sorry he'd missed work and would be taking a couple of weeks off due to some private medical issues concerning his wife. After she wrapped up her current piece, he'd message her regarding her next assignment in the coming days. She put the phone on the desk and went back to her research.

One of the final pieces she found on him was from ten years ago. A small article out of a Manila newspaper. Apparently, after Severin's retirement, he had spent some time in developing countries, volunteering his expertise helping low-income patients receive transplant heart surgeries. His last documented mission of mercy was on the island of Mindanao. Not much else on him after that time. Then, according to public records, he simply returned to Los Angeles, leased out a studio, and stayed quiet. That was five years ago.

No reports about his advanced jaundice or any other medical conditions. He had kept his illness private. Thyroid issues, pancreatitis, cancer– she could only speculate.

Yazmina slouched over her desk and rubbed her cheek. She understood the point of the Body Booth; that it was meant to trigger some sort of guilt response in participants, but she didn't understand *Severin*. Why did he want people to experience these things? She looped back through the digital recorder. He mentioned several benefactors wanting anonymity. Perhaps there had been no point. Perhaps it was just a game for bored men.

Her phone vibrated again. An unlisted call.

"Hello?"

"Ms. Mejia."

"Why are—"

"I'm hosting an impromptu exhibit with some of my closest friends. Tomorrow night at eight. Maybe you'd like to get their perspectives for your piece."

She couldn't resist something like that. And maybe he knew it, too.

"I'll…be there."

"Good. And please, tell no one."

A butler wearing a black balaclava greeted her at the door with a thin smile and a serving tray. He handed her a glass of Champagne.

"Oh, I can't drink," she said, taking the drink, more from fear than good manners.

The man smiled and walked away.

Beethoven's Moonlight Sonata played from concealed overhead speakers as a dozen men in balaclavas and finely tailored tuxedos mingled in the studio, wide-eyed, the din of their chatter buzzing electric. This group was experiencing the Body Booth for the first time.

She shot a sidelong glance at the booth. The outer dermis of its panels appeared to wilt and turn pale. The doors were shut. Someone had been taking a turn.

Severin approached her and held out his hand. "Hello, Ms. Mejia."

Yazmina shook his hand. It was cold, clammy. "Doctor."

"Thank you for coming. I have spoken to these men about you. They have agreed to answer your questions. But as you can see, anonymity is paramount."

"And why, may I ask, is that?"

"You've experienced my creation. Anyone who hasn't would surely view everyone in this room as depraved. These are men of distinction and have reputations to uphold. They wouldn't want to be persecuted for their tastes. Now, if you'll excuse me."

With that, he turned away and shambled behind the booth.

As she waded deeper into the studio, she felt their eyes fall on her, her belly. It wasn't lost on her that she was the only woman in the room. A knot formed in her stomach. That familiar dread. She'd felt it before in the presence of narcos. Back in Ciudad Juárez when she had interviewed low-level cartel enforcers, anonymous, masked, just like this.

Something off-putting about clandestine societies. Men and their exclusive clubs. Their secrets. In her experience, nothing good ever came from it.

She approached the closest person to her; a tall, slender man drifting from the rest of the pack.

"Hello, I'm Yazmina Mejia from *The Times*. Would I be able to ask you a few questions?"

The man took a sip of his Champagne. "That would be alright."

Yasmina fumbled around in her bag for her recorder.

"No recordings," the man said.

Her cheeks flushed. "Of course, sorry." She set her glass on the floor and retrieved a pen and notebook. "Alright. May I ask your profession?"

"I'm a teacher at a private school." He took another sip, his eyes accosting her.

She jotted his response. "And have you experienced the Body Booth?"

The man lifted his sleeve, flashing his bandaged wrist.

"What are your thoughts on this so called 'art installation?' Your experience?"

The man bent forward and leaned in close to her ear. "It's an abomination. If I could, I'd set fire to it." He eyed her bulging belly. "If I were you, I would forget the whole thing and leave." He straightened up, rolled down his sleeve, and turned away.

She lifted her glass and continued to pace around the room, gauging faces, body language. Most men's eyes would dart away as she approached. Like nervous schoolboys with a crush. Or who had been guilty of mischief.

The doors to the booth parted, a man stepped out, blood spotting through his bandaged hand. The dermis on the panels flushed as blood pumped through their cells again.

She approached the man and blocked his path. "Hello, I'm Yazmina—"

"I know who you are."

Yazmina thought the man's voice familiar but she couldn't quite pin it down. She gazed into his eyes; burning blue orbs, familiar yet foreign.

"May I ask your profession?"

The man pursed his lips, looked cautiously around the room before answering. "I'm an actor."

"I see," she said. Perhaps he'd been in a movie she'd seen. Or a daytime soap opera. The roots of this secret society ran deep. "What was your experience? What are your thoughts on the Body Booth?"

The actor shut his eyes and tilted his head back. A junkie in the thralls of ecstasy. "It's a fucking rush. A goddamn wonder." The actor opened his eyes, flashed his pearly whites, and zipped past her.

Yazmina stood there, gazing at the open double doors, past its maw, and into the throbbing panels of gastric lining. She felt its pull. Calling her. *A goddamn wonder*. Without a second thought, she stepped inside and shut the doors.

She set her bag underneath the counter and placed a gentle hand on a fleshy panel, felt its viscous, slimy texture, the small crypts of its honeycombed membranes, the contours of its bulges, the raised bumps of its snaking veins and blood vessels.

It was no doubt a marvel. A revolting one at that. A nightmarish hybrid of abstract art, antiquated technology, and modern science. But in it, she found a kind of beauty, pulsing gently through its blood vessels. How could this thing not be alive? She ran a hand along an exposed thin metal beam where the flesh hadn't grown. Its tissue had grown like moss, overtaking the bones of something now considered dead, obsolete.

Perhaps it was curiosity that led her to it, but she dipped two fingers into the glass of Champagne and pressed them to the booth. Every panel writhed and puckered and shriveled until the flesh became a thin, gray necrotic hide.

Yazmina gasped and dropped the glass, sending up a storm of crystalline shards, splashing alcohol over her legs. "Oh my God! Nononono."

She snatched the scalpel from the counter and sliced deep into her left palm, shearing through the bandaging. Grunting, she placed her weeping hand against the flesh and massaged it in soft, circular motions. The cilia brushed up along her skin and probed deep into the gash. "There, there," Yazmina whispered, "everything is alright. Everything is alright."

As before, the tissue ceased its writhing. Its rosy color returned as it bloated and filled with her blood.

The memory of pain returned as her wound flared. Yazmina eyed her hand. Blood pumped rhythmically from the incision. It was deep this time. She would need stitches.

Brrriiinnngggg. The phone rang. Startled, she nearly jumped. *Brrriiinnngggg*. She regarded it, vibrating on the cradle. Did no one else hear it? *Brrriiinnngggg*.

Outside, she heard muffled chatter, laughter. Were they playing a prank on her? *Brrriiinnngggg*. She picked up the phone, and brought it to her ear.

"Thank you," the voice said before the line went dead.

She was dreaming of a baby; sexless, mewling, its skin blue and ashen like a corpse. It called to her with outstretched arms and chubby, grasping fingers. *Hungry*. As she neared, lifting her shirt to nurse it, it bared a row of sharp teeth and black, necrotic gums. She reeled, tried to flee, but found herself tethered to it through a rapidly shrinking umbilical cord.

Yazmina yanked on the cord, planted her feet, tried to push off and break away. But the more she struggled, the quicker she found herself being dragged toward the baby. Soon, the space between them shrunk and their bellies pressed together. Little by little she got sucked into the abomination's naval until she had become completely absorbed and there was only darkness.

Her phone rang.

She opened her eyes and was met with the same darkness. Her hands probed blindly for the phone on the nightstand. She squinted as the light shone on her face.

Unlisted number.

"Hello?"

There was only the sound of slow, labored breathing, like a gust blowing through the mouth of a cave.

"Who is this?"

Click.

She felt the baby kick. "It's okay, Kiki. Everything is okay." She sat up and massaged her belly. A comfort as much to herself as to Kiki. That the nightmare was just that. As for that call…

Her left palm began to itch. Badly. Yazmina unwound the fresh bandaging Severin had applied. She looked over her hand. Six stitches ran along the length of the gape in her palm like barbed wire. No need to involve the hospital, he'd assured her.

She scratched the wound gently. Severin told her not to touch it but she couldn't help it. The itch was unbearable, the sensation, like a swarm of ants crawling under her skin. And there was pain. The flesh around her wound felt raw and tender. What had she done to herself? She'd given in to the thing, unthinking. Like instinct.

There was another pang in her belly. Not a contraction or a kick. But guilt. That was it. Her thoughts settled on the booth, the living tissue, alone at night in its cold chamber. Unloved. She found it hard to believe herself, but the thought had gnawed at her, knowing it would perish if uncared for. What if there was ever an accident and the blood drip became detached? Would it suffer? Would it die quickly?

No. She shook her head. Severin had said it didn't have pain receptors or something to that effect. Then again, how would he know whether it could or couldn't feel pain? She needed to learn more about the Body Booth. What DNA

159

he'd used to create the thing. What Severin's end goal was. Would it be a permanent fixture at his studio? Forever destined to crave blood, to be unfulfilled? Was its fate truly tied to the whims of every individual in its presence?

Her phone rang.

Unlisted number. Again.

She knew better than to answer but she wanted to tell whoever was calling to leave her alone.

"Hello?"

"Ms. Mejia," Severin said. "I'm afraid you forgot your bag at the studio."

"Shit," Yazmina said. After Severin had sewn her up, she'd left in a hurry. Her wallet, her recorder, her work ID. All of it in the bag.

Fuck. Had he discovered the recorder?

"Doctor, is there any way I can get that from you tonight?"

"Of course. Feel free to drop by."

She looked at the time. Half-past-midnight. The baby kicked, a sharp protest that made Yazmina wince.

"I'll be there in twenty minutes."

"Hello, Doctor," Yazmina said, breathless from the arduous walk down the hallway. The stress of carrying Kiki around had begun to take its toll on her feet, ankles, and knees as she'd grown larger.

"Ms. Mejia," Severin said from behind the door. His yellow face had been partly obscured by a web of shadows on account of the dimmed lights. Behind him, toward the center of the room, the Body Booth sat under the dual crossed beams of the overhead lamps. "You really should be more mindful."

She nodded. "I appreciate you taking the time. Where's my bag?"

"Right where you left it," he said, pulling the door wide. He swept a hand toward the booth. "Feel free."

Yazmina felt unease. It was late and no one had known she was here. Not even Francis. She had no choice.

"Okay. I'll be getting it now." She padded into the studio, the wooden floorboards bowing and creaking under her weight like a moaning beast.

A piercing hum emanated from the booth. A constant droning that hung in the air.

The refrigeration unit, perhaps. The blood drip keeping the gastric tissue alive. She hadn't noticed it before, but now, in the quiet of the night, it was almost deafening.

She parted the doors open.

Inside, everything appeared darker than it had before. Perhaps her eyes hadn't adjusted yet. But the bag was sitting under the counter's shadow, right where she'd left it. She picked up the bag, strapped it over her shoulder, and turned to leave.

Cilia began to sprout from every fleshy pore, stiffening, pointing in Yazmina's direction. Like antennae sensing the air of its environment. Or grasping. Pleading. *Hungry*.

One last time.

The scalpel sat where it always had, waiting for her. Just a small one. She nicked the tip of her thumb and squeezed until blood began to weep from the wound. She tilted her head, lifted her hand above her shoulders, and pressed her hand to the ceiling. Strands of cilia caressed her thumb, rubbing up and down her skin, following the contours of the grooves in her fingerprints. Exploring her.

There was something she hadn't noticed. A melon-sized sac of flesh, much like a cocoon or a hornet's nest, growing over the blue overhead light, which was now dim and scantly visible. She could feel a hint of the light's warmth radiating through the leathery film. She slid a gentle finger across the sac. It jerked at her touch.

"Everything okay?" Severin's voice startled her, jostling her backward so that her hip bumped against the counter. He stood at the mouth of the booth, hands crossed behind his back.

"There's a lump of flesh growing over the light. It wasn't there before."

Severin followed her gaze. "Mm. Cellular overgrowth. Gastrointestinal stromal tumor, perhaps."

"Like cancer?"

"Possibly. I can't be sure without a biopsy."

Yasmina shuffled out of the booth, nudging past Severin. "The cilia acted differently toward me. It seemed to be playful. As if it recognized me."

"Procedural memory. It's only responding to positive stimuli. That's all."

She nodded and made her way toward the door. Once in the hallway, she turned to Severin one last time. "Doctor? Why blood?"

"Sometimes you need to find the right medium to tell a story." A smile cut across his face. His face looked deteriorated. He had been nearing the end. "The Body Booth is a canvas. Every canvas needs paint spilled on its surface. And the right artist to make it happen."

Something was wrong. A stillness had overcome her body; something she couldn't discern. She felt the warmth of the sun on her face, stirring her from her slumber. When she opened her eyes, she woke to blood-stained sheets. Quickly, she sat upright. Her thighs rubbed together, wet and sticky. She slid a hand down her legs and drew back blood. Dark. Dry. She pressed a hand to her stomach and held it, waiting to feel a sign from Kiki.

Nothing.

The technician didn't make eye contact as she wiped the gel from Yazmina's belly. She told her she could get dressed now, that her doctor would see her shortly. As Yazmina buttoned her blouse, a profound feeling of guilt and grief washed over her. As if something were lost. A part of her that would never return.

She hadn't even registered the doctor knocking on the door before she'd entered the room. The world had become a hazy, fragmented dream. A mirage. Nothing was real. Nothing made sense.

The doctor placed a hand on Yazmina's shoulder. Used phrases like *fetal death in utero. Placental abruption. Arterial bleeding. Rare occurrence.*

Yazmina nodded absentmindedly. An automatic response. The doctor told her that they could begin inducing labor immediately.

The world became blurry as a film of tears covered Yazmina's eyes. The furniture, the doctor; all became abstracts of their former selves. She told the doctor she wanted more time. To say goodbye.

Despite her concerns for Yazmina's emotional state, the doctor reassured her she could safely induce labor naturally in a few weeks.

That evening she thrashed in bed, wailing, pulling the bloody bedsheets up to her face. She inhaled, hoping to extract some essence from her daughter. To breathe her in, know her scent before it faded forever.

She screamed into her pillow. Who would she confide in now? Who would she pen poems for? Who would she read bedtime stories to? Thoughts drifted to the half-assembled crib. A casket for a ghost and nothing more.

The phone rang. And rang. She made no attempt to answer. She was happy to lie there, an undead thing straddling life and oblivion. By the fifth attempt, she had grown furious at the intrusions. She just wanted her privacy. Just her and her daughter and nothing more. Kiki.

It rang a sixth time.

She answered.

"Ms. Mejia," Severin said.

She said nothing.

"Word has travelled about your misfortune. I am so sorry. I am arranging another gathering tonight at eight. I invite you. Not as a journalist but as a friend. So you won't be alone."

Yazmina hung up.

For some ungodly amount of time, she just lay there, staring at the ceiling as the world grew dark. She was alone and cold, in need of embrace and understanding. Like the booth.

She forced herself out of bed and got dressed. Then she drove downtown.

The same butler from before opened the door and motioned her inside, a polite smile painting his masked face.

Severin stood beside the booth, tending to his guests. As she stepped inside, the audience turned to face her, all wearing false smiles under black masks. Masks within masks.

The Body Booth stood where it always had, pale skin pressed up against its double glass doors. Awaiting her touch. Her nurture.

Its pull drew her in. She began, almost catatonically, making her way toward the booth. Though she didn't look down at her feet, she felt almost as if she were gliding over the floor. Light as a feather.

A dozen shrouded men in tuxedos parted aside, clearing her path. They ogled her. She felt their eyes falling on her belly like hungry jackals.

Severin swept a hand toward the booth, smiling, inviting. As she opened the doors, she glanced at the new placard which read:

Andrzej Severin, M.D.

American, 1950-

Mother and Child

Gastrointestinal Tissue on Telephone Booth and Human Female

Yazmina stepped inside, not caring to shut the doors behind her. As the crowd swarmed the doors, she placed both hands on a fleshy panel, feeling the cilia pushing back, bristling her skin in concentric strokes. The sensation was stimulating, her nerve endings flaring euphorically. The touch of a loved one.

Yazmina softly tipped her forehead to the wall. She felt a warmth that hadn't been there before. She allowed it to fill her. To make her smile.

The gastric flesh squirmed and shriveled and began to lose color. The heat of its touch dissipated. Yazmina felt a tremendous pang in her gut and she shrieked in pain. She braced her arms along the dying walls for support as her insides tore apart. Her legs trembled as the stillborn thing inside her began to pass through her body.

She breathed in and out, pushing rhythmically until the baby spilled out of her; tiny and bloody and slimy and withered and lifeless. It had ashen-blue skin. Nothing but a prune. She lifted the child, which was still attached to her through a knotted cord, and cradled it in the crook of her arm. She raised the baby toward a fleshy panel. The cilia accepted its offering, enveloping the remains of what once had a name.

The baby disappeared into that forest of overbearing follicles. There came a crunch and the sound of something wet. The tissue began to regain its rosy color, throbbing as it processed its meal.

There was a tug between her thighs. Burning. The stomach walls began to contract like a muscle as it pulled her by the umbilical cord, the cilia stabbing at it like a thousand sickles. She planted her feet on the rusted floor and began to pedal backward, but her legs wobbled, weak, spent. The booth drew her in. Her belly pressed against the cilia and she screamed as she felt the flaring pain of a thousand miniscule eviscerations. Blood poured freely from the tears on her torso.

The fleshy sac above her head began to rupture strand by sinuous strand, its fissures seeping torrents of viscous, gastric jelly. Before she passed out, Yazmina heard the garbled, muffled cries of something inside.

Doctor Andrzej Severin smiled; his piece completed.

The men applauded as she gave life to art.

Postcards from Saguaroland

1.

Like television static in the middle of the night, visions of aberrant shapes flickered in and out of Gustavo's mind as he dreamed. He stood alone on an expanse of barren land baring only gnarled, dead roots and dry shrubs bristling in a breeze. Something pulled his gaze toward the night sky. Akin to rustling behind a black curtain there were forms—or the hints of forms—skulking in the darkness between the stars. He wanted desperately to look away.

Before he could turn, a hail of meteorites plunged to Earth, the cosmic scattershot strangely inaudible as it decimated the desert landscape. Curious, he took two paces forward. A throng of squirming monstrosities burst from beneath charred, glassy craters. Under the faint glow of moonlight, he could discern only the vaguest of features. Their shapes were amorphous, their extremities gelatinous and pallid and covered in oozing polyps. They scurried forth, thin stalks sprouting from their bodies upon which countless obsidian eyes blinked in tandem. Though they bore no mouths, he knew they were coming to feast upon his flesh.

Gustavo opened his eyes, woken by the cold sting at the small of his back. His eyes adjusted and the dark, vast desert greeted him. Only the world was upside down.

Nearby, a cluster of saguaros stood watch, their long limbs menacing in the shadows.

His brain slogged through a haze; he couldn't remember what had happened or how he'd gotten here.

Something punctured his skin before it sheared through the length of his spine, stopping just shy of his shoulder blades. He screamed, the pain flaring throughout his body like a sweeping fire. Instinctively, he tried to flail his arms but a glance proved his wrists were bound below his head, his fingers wriggling not more than four feet from a patch of dry desert scrub.

Like syrup, something warm and wet ran along his bare back and past his neck, finally soaking into the tangle of disheveled hair. He tilted his head so that his chin pressed against his chest. Above, thick strands of rope bound his ankles to a shoddy-looking gibbet.

A swell of blood rushed to his head, thrumming to the beat of his heart before cold perspiration trickled down his temples. He had come to know this torture device from his time in another country. When he had been a different person and under the employ of questionable men. Only, he had been on the opposite end of the scaffolding then.

Cold fingers clutched his hamstring and turned him slowly around. Emily Brentwood stood over him, a large blood-stained hunting knife in her hand. A warm smile had been etched across her pale face. Beside her, Dillan Jacob held a torch, the flames illuminating his expressionless face in a raging red light. There were a dozen others he didn't recognize. Gringos like them.

Behind them, a small mob regarded his swaying body like children watching a magician pull a string of cards from his mouth. They were garbed in braids and colorful dresses; in cowboy hats, tight blue jeans, and leather boots. Gustavo recognized their tanned faces from town. The *abuela* with braids. The stone-faced man behind the wheel of the pickup truck. The little girls from the alley. They were his compatriotas. His countrymen. Only something was off.

It was then he thought he saw movement, something shifting on their faces. *Under* their faces. He narrowed his eyes; small eyeholes appeared to be cut out of their heads like Halloween masks. Behind the cavities, black, beady pinholes rolled about, staring back, the skin underneath them pale, glistening, writhing.

He gazed across the desert, looking for someone, anyone that could help. Not more than a few hundred feet behind the mob, the amber lights of the warehouse parking lot flickered like fireflies. He licked his lips and tried calling out for help.

No words came. A powerful gust blew in. The air nipped at his skin, cooling the blood at his back and turning the hairs on his body prickly like cactus needles. The saguaro themselves swayed delicately side-to-side. But those looked peculiar, too. Under the faint glow of the torch's fire, he thought he glimpsed the impressions of flayed, strung-up corpses.

Emily stepped behind him and slid the knife up his back again, the incision ending at the base of his skull. He shrieked and watched a trail of vapor fade into the night sky where the stars didn't flicker, like unblinking eyes.

"They came from the darkness between the galaxies," she said softly into his ear while laying a gentle, frigid hand upon his cheek. "Not by choice, but here we are."

Gustavo felt control over his limbs slip away as they shivered uncontrollably. He knew he was going into shock.

"Their flesh was not meant for the harshness of our sun."

Though his back was starting to numb, he thought he felt, briefly, a scorching sensation radiate along his back. His mind tried to make sense of what he'd been feeling and his imagination drifted into abysmal places. He pictured her nailed fingers plunging into his spine and pulling the skin from his muscle.

"They have asked us to provide them with tinted skins so that they may know the pleasures of walking uninhibited among our world."

"Tinted s-skins?" Gustavo stammered through chattering teeth. He coughed; his every breath more labored than the last. He thought about people that looked like him. Hundreds trekked into border towns like this every day. He thought about his boys, their brown, ashy skin being peeled away.

The postcard. What had he done? His eyes welled with tears, obscuring the world around him.

"More are already on their way. Can you hear them? The song of the Pallid Ones grows louder."

Gustavo heard only the shuffling of feet dragging over gravel in the distance. Slowly, the scraping grew louder, jarring in the silence of the desert. He craned his neck. Something vile approached. It was the color of a cold, dead cadaver, its skin gleaming with something slick and moist.

As the distorted thing neared the light of the torch, the flesh on Gustavo's back tingled. *No.* He shook his head and shut his eyes so hard they hurt. It was all he could do.

167

He wept. This couldn't be real. Things like this only happened in dreams.

2.

Gustavo woke abruptly inside the sedan, simultaneously bracing his left hand against the driver's side window while slamming his foot on the brake pedal. Once he'd realized that the car had been parked, he eased up and sighed. *Idiot.*

The dream had been terrifying, he knew that much, though the details had already evaporated into the ether. He was only certain that his head was pounding. He rubbed his temples and glared at the empty tequila bottle on the mat. For a moment he had forgotten where he had been. Everything came back as soon as he peered out the smudged window. It was the same dull border town, the buildings still small and unimposing, the tinted windows from local shops etched with the scrawl of old graffiti. The paint on most buildings had faded, washed out by the light of an oppressive sun. The foundations appeared to be sinking into the Sonoran Desert, soon to be swallowed whole and forgotten like every outpost he'd driven through. It was the kind of cookie cutter oasis found along the highways of the American Southwest. Except this place had been different. This place really was a refuge.

Gustavo got out and stretched. The sun began its descent over some low-lying hills on the western horizon, its fading light casting long blue shadows across the boulevard. He looked at his watch. There was still time.

He ambled up Main Street for half a block until he came upon a phone booth. He dug out some change and dropped a dollar's worth of quarters through the slot.

As far as children went, Carlitos and Hector were two of the loveliest boys a father could've been gifted. Though, he wasn't sure they thought so highly of him. Not anymore. And Sandra. Well, he knew what his wife thought of him. He tried to convince them, and himself, that leaving was for the best. Things had gotten too dangerous for him to stay. Besides, there would be good jobs on the other side and he could wire them money. But sometimes plans had a way of dying premature deaths.

How long had it been since he had heard their voices? He had stopped counting the days for some time. Since the money dried up. Gustavo cradled the phone between his face and shoulder. His hands trembled as his finger hovered over the grimy keypad. He had rehearsed the speech dozens of times during those long, lonely drives though empty stretches of highway. He knew he'd say that he loved them. That he was really going to straighten up his act this time. But now he had found a town that offered decent work and welcomed people that looked like them. Soon, their troubles would be over and he would be able to send for them across the border. No more begging gringos for change at the crossing line. No more watered-down charro bean dinners. He punched in his old phone number.

The line was dead.

His heart sank into his belly and he swallowed a hard lump that may as well have been a stone. Seldom existed worse tortures in this life than broken promises.

He hung up and shoved two fingers into the coin release slot. It was empty.

A pickup truck ambled down the street, its driver, a sullen-looking Mexican man in a cowboy hat, eyed him suspiciously from the dark of the cab. Gustavo broke eye contact and kept on.

On the walk back to the car he stopped to gaze at his reflection on a tinted window. He was looking gaunt, thinner than he remembered. Even his skin had tanned considerably from those long days driving through the desert. He ran a hand through his greasy black hair, doing his best to part it neatly in the middle. Then he wiped the crust from his bloodshot eyes. He looked like shit but it was the best he was going to look for a while. At least until he could find a place of his own with a shower. He looked at the signage above. *Jacob Drugstore.*

Gustavo peered through the open door. A small spinning rack atop the counter contained a collection of postcards.

Inside, a young blonde cashier no older than eighteen flashed a smile that beckoned him forth. Gustavo shuffled inside.

"Hey, amigo" the cashier said. "Name's Dillan Jacob. I'm covering for my pop so let me know if you need any help."

Gustavo nodded. "Just going to take a quick look," he said. He spun the rack, gazing at everything from ephemeral collages to postcards with local Southwest-themed artwork.

He plucked one that caught his eye: A colorful abstract oil painting of the open desert, majestic saguaros seemingly waving their arms in welcome. *Greetings from Saguaroland.*

"I'll take this one and enough postage to send this to Mexico," Gustavo said, sliding the man his last twenty.

"Of course," Dillan said, ringing him up and handing him his change. "Great pick."

"Do you have a pen?"

Dillan smiled again, handing him a blue ballpoint.

Gustavo printed his old address on the back of the card. *Please, God, tell me they still live there.* He scribbled a quick note: *If you can make it here, find me. Sending my love. Gustavo Luna.*

It's all he could do now.

"I can mail that for you," Dillan said eagerly. "Mailman comes this way in about half an hour."

Gustavo looked up at him, considered his offer for a moment, and nodded. "Thank you, my friend."

"My pleasure, amigo. We're all here to help."

Outside, the sun had vanished behind inky hills. He made his way back to the car and opened the atlas. The location of the warehouse had been marked in red ink, just beyond the old train tracks on the southern edge of town.

He started the car. The streets gave way to dirt roads as the town faded in his rearview mirror. The wash of light pollution gradually receded and the desert grew darker and wider. On either side of road, the silhouettes of saguaros reached out for him like desperate marionettes. He wasn't sure if they were pleading for help or trying to swallow him whole like voracious monsters.

The car rumbled past the tracks. Ahead, the warehouse loomed behind a barbed wire fence, its corrugated exterior depressing and stark under the light of the stars. Tonight, he would start a new chapter. He wouldn't mess this up. Not for anything in the world. He pulled into the warm amber glow of the parking lot.

3.

The morning sun beat down on Gustavo Luna's face as he stepped out of the car, its light especially cruel and blinding. He shielded his eyes with both hands and surveyed his new surroundings.

As far as he could tell it was a small town dotted with liquor stores, gas stations, mobile homes, and janky watering holes. On either side of town, the Sonoran Desert stretched into the horizon. Nothing but crumbling highway billboards, towering saguaros, dry scrub, and dirt. Heaps and heaps of dirt. It had probably all been unincorporated land nestled along the Mexican border.

Gustavo had come across countless places like this, though some had been affixed to prairies or snow-covered valleys. In his experience, they were all the same. Each town had its share of drunkards, dullards, or unwelcoming bigots. There were always the kind ones too, but those were getting rarer these days. There hadn't been much on the jobs front in any of them, either. Not for someone like him. He supposed there were always big cities but those posed the biggest danger. Too many people. Too many eyes. He wasn't about to be shipped back to a country that chewed you up and spat you out a killer or poorer than when you first went in. He wondered how his boys were doing and bit his lip. Wherever they were he hoped they knew that he was trying his best.

He leaned over the atlas on the hood of the car and traced his finger along the last route he had taken. Where had he gotten lost? He shook his head. Maybe he'd dozed off, taken a wrong turn somewhere. Wherever he was, it wasn't on the map. He covered his mouth to stifle a yawn. His eyes felt heavy and dry. It felt like he had been driving for ages. A dark journey of never-ending blacktop. He folded up the atlas and tried to gather his bearings. He stood near the corner of Main Street and Rawlins, which appeared to be the town's main hub; all thrift shops, convenient stores, and tax service centers. It would be as good a place as any to start.

A terrible scent wafted on a warm current of air. He covered his mouth and fought the urge to wretch right there on the street. Flies hovered ravenously over something lodged in a storm drain just beside the car. The anomaly was opaque, its flesh cancerous, like a dead jellyfish swathed in small, bubbling cysts. He prodded the thing with his shoe and the flies scattered. Nothing but a plastic bag crawling with maggots, its insides filled with something moist and rotten. He decided he didn't want to know.

His car's engine ticked as it struggled to cool in the sunlight and he thought he could use some cooling off too. He hopped up on the sidewalk and took refuge under the shade of an awning.

Next, he would do the usual and go door-to-door inquiring about jobs until it was time to pack it in and leave. He'd likely be told the same thing: *Sorry, amigo. No trabajo. No work here.*

An old brown woman in braids glared at him behind a barred window in her home across the street before drawing the curtains shut. She reminded him of his abuela and better days.

He sauntered down the street, eyeing the local shops and businesses for any Help Wanted signs but everything was bust. Halfway down the street a pair of dark-skinned girls in matching pink shirts gawked at him from the maw of a darkened alley. He waved. They turned and scampered into the shadows. So, his gente were here. A welcome sight. But the odd stares. They were likely wary of strangers like he was. Always on guard. He didn't blame them. You never knew who was going to turn you over to the migra. There was nothing promised about the Promised Land. Any day could be your last here.

Something caught his attention just aways down the block. The large signage painted on the front of an unassuming building at the end of the street was hard to miss: *Saguaroland Staffing Agency.*

He half-jogged there and wiped the sweat from his brow with the back of his hand. It was a dusty beige building with cracking walls and dented venetian blinds, not too unlike the rest of the town's aesthetic. Inside, the cool conditioned air was a welcome relief on his warm skin. A pale, blonde woman behind a desk smiled through ruby lips and waved him over.

"Welcome, amigo," she said. "How can I help you?"

Gustavo cleared his throat. "I saw your sign. I am looking for work."

"Well, come on in," she said sweeping her hand over a chair in front of her desk. "My name's Emily Brentwood, by the way."

"Gustavo Luna," he said, sitting down. Besides Emily, the office was empty. A muted television set mounted on a corner wall played a news segment about the alarming rise of missing people in the state. Which state? He wasn't exactly sure where he was just yet.

"A pleasure." She reached into a drawer and retrieved a few forms.

"I don't have papers," he interrupted. He looked at his mud-caked shoes, his fingers tapping anxiously on the table.

Emily placed her hands over his. They were cold but soft. Sincere. Gustavo blushed, suddenly self-conscious of the missing pinky on his left hand and the tattooed knuckles on his right. He peered up. Her eyes had already settled where he didn't want them to and he pulled away. They were scars from another life. Like an itch, he wanted to shed his old skin and molt into another. Had it been possible to be two different people in a single lifespan?

He hoped she didn't ask about the markings.

She didn't.

"You have very strong hands, Gustavo. There's an opening for an overnight position at a warehouse just outside of town. They could use a guy like you."

"But—"

172

"All under the table." She winked. "We get lots of undocumented laborers around these parts. We consider ourselves something of a sanctuary town."

Gustavo eased back into the chair and smiled. It had been the first time in ages.

"Now, the job is minimum wage but you can expect quarterly raises if they decide to keep you. Can you start tonight?"

"Yes, of course!" Moisture started to pool under his eyes. He couldn't believe a word of it. He wanted to call his children and share the news. In time, the nightmare would be over. The terrors of poverty, the cartels, of lives unfulfilled began to look more and more like an obstacle that could be surmounted with time and care and patience.

"Please don't cry," she said smiling once more through bleached teeth. "Everything will be okay. I promise."

Gustavo wiped the tears from his eyes and nodded.

Emily scribbled an address on the back of a business card and slid it across the table.

"It's just over the train tracks," she said. "They're going to love you."

He wanted to hug her. The world suddenly looked a little brighter. This truly was a land of opportunity. Of redemption.

He smiled again. This couldn't be real. Things like this only happened in dreams.

Story Notes

"Nightmare of a Million Faces"
This story was inspired by the assault on women's rights and the lack of agency women are usually allowed to wield in this world. Women face battles men typically don't, such as reproductive rights. Some women are forced to give birth, others are forced to abort. Many times, their government or their partners don't give them a say in the matter. Many women in relationships are victims of emotional and physical abuse and feel powerless to speak out for fear of safety or that no one will believe them. This story touches on some of those matters, some by way of internal fears, and some external. Anastasia driving out into the desert in the middle of the night was my attempt to depict how alone someone can feel when faced with these terrors. A big influence on this story was also my friend and mentor, Dennis Etchison, whose tales of lonely roadside travelers have made a huge impact on my writing. This is one of many cosmic horror stories in this collection, which is a subgenre I love to toil in.

"Feast of the Dreamer"
Haven't we all had it so rough we conjured up a dream world to help us escape what haunts us? That's what I envisioned for this ex-sicario on the run from his former employers and the ghosts of those he's wronged. I have a fascination with the cartels thar run much of Mexico. They are violent, brutal, and merciless in their

targeting of rivals, journalists, and dissenters. I've often wondered if the narcos have grown numb to the trail of blood they've left behind, or if by chance, a few of them still feel slivers of remorse for their sins, such as the sicario in this story. But this character takes this situation to a ghoulish extreme when he cannibalizes the dead in the hopes his meals will induce a hallucinatory world where he could escape the terrors that haunt him. This story was based on something that happened to me, when I experienced food poisoning so severe, I ran a fever and began to hear voices in my head telling me to kill myself.

"Skins"
I've always thought that the illicit hunting of baby seals was a cruel and horrifying practice. Putting myself in their position, being out on the ice, vulnerable to humans, their weapons, and their ill intents made me think of this scenario. The story: What would happen if humans were to experience a similar fate?

"Shantytown: A Mexican Ghost Story"
Children see the world through a very particular lens, certainly different than how adults view it. Things that may seem mundane to adults like curtains flapping in the night may seem menacing or frightening to younger eyes. In this story, Maribel, a little girl living in a shantytown in Tijuana, bears witness to things like shadow people, monsters, and the dead they leave in their wake, which are stand-ins for cartel violence. It is also a pointed social critique of the Mexican government in its failure to tackle the cartels, as well as a critique of American manufacturers which operate near shantytowns like this and pollute the local environment.

"Purveyors and Puppets"
This story was inspired by the political news pundits and ideologues on nightly television that spew their manufactured vitriol, sowing the seeds of hate, xenophobia, and distrust for their public to consume. Sometimes their hate spills out through real-life acts of violence, committed by people so invested in their lies and rhetoric, that they see other humans as mortal enemies. I took that concept and created this story, putting it through a nihilistic, cosmic horror lens.

"Roots in Kon Tum"
The U.S. caused ecological damage during the Vietnam War when it dispensed

chemical agents as part of its herbicidal warfare program. Weaponized chemicals like Agent Orange, for instance, were used as defoliants, but also caused severe illnesses like cancer or birth defects in millions of victims. This is a story of the poisoned land taking revenge on a veteran who has returned in an attempt to absolve his sins during the war.

"Midnight Frequencies"
Taco truck vendors put up with some weird people in the odd hours of the night, especially in big cities: drunk folk, belligerent people, even armed robbers. It's also about the difficulty of making the right decisions while trying to make a better life. This story amps up those scenarios when a very carnivorous extraterrestrial species makes planetfall in the heart of Downtown Los Angeles. I thought of these alien invaders as something of food tourists. Very dangerous ones.

"The Cellar"
Siblings trapped in a raging California wildfire seek shelter in an abandoned cellar, wherein resides a cosmic being that stuns its prey by inducing dreams through psychoactive spores. A twisted take on the Wizard of Oz. This story also tackles grief and how it latches onto our conscious and follows us all our lives. Sometimes that anguish can be our biggest enemy.

"The Savage Night"
I always wanted to write a neolithic horror story. This is it. It features a unique take on the origin of a much-feared monster we all know: the vampire. Also, this story touches thematically on loneliness and the horrifying results of desperation. According to editor Ann van de Bergh, who originally published this story, it felt like a mix of Robert E. Howard, Philip Jose Farmer, and a dash of Jack London. I'll take it.

"The Bottom-Dweller"
Editor Ben Thomas had the wonderful idea of creating an anthology based on a shuttered theme park that never was. A theme park where mysterious, uncanny, and frightening things tended to happen. This is one of those stories. A nautical tale of terror steeped in cosmic horror roots.

"Adrift Ebon Tides"
Another nautical cosmic horror story. Two men stranded at sea in the dead of night when things get weird. Bleak, nihilistic, short and sweet. Some big influences on my work are authors like H.P. Lovecraft, Thomas Ligotti, Laird Barron, and John Langan. There's something about nihilistic cosmic horror that speaks to me on such a profound level. The air of mystery, of the unknowable, of the knowledge that life may have no meaning, and the chill of learning that the terrors that stalk you are as eternal and uncaring as the cosmos themselves.

"Midnight Shoeshine"
A story set on the Santa Monica Pier just after the Great Depression. A man who has lost everything is about to throw himself into the ocean. Can life get any worse? Perhaps. It was fun to dabble in one of the bleakest time periods in U.S. history.

"The Last Train out of Calico"
A western horror that takes place on a speeding train, set just outside Calico, California in the Mojave Desert. It's a real-life ghost town you can visit on the way to Las Vegas from L.A. I love Westerns, and, again, I dabbled in cosmic horror for this one. The creature here was inspired by the spider crabs I'd catch as a kid when I'd go fishing with my dad. He'd set up a net at the end of the pier and cast it over with a long line of rope. Those things looked otherworldly with their craggy, rocky-looking shells and spindly legs as they clambered over one another. This one was fun to write and includes a diverse cast of misfits and bandidos, which is seldom seen in Westerns.

"Bad Dogs"
A mother with drug addiction issues finds herself stranded alongside her toddler on questionable streets one rainy night. Alone and desperate, she seeks shelter in an old telephone booth. Outside, shapes move about in the darkness, shapes resembling upright, lupine creatures. I toyed with ambiguity here as it was more about the introspective journey the mother had to embark on, a journey of self-discovery and finding what lengths she'd venture to protect her daughter. Even if it means killing old habits.

"Birthday Boy"
This was my most Brian Evenson-esque story. It's weird. I once again revisit the

177

theme of cartel violence, and again, I do it through a child's eyes. This particularly deals with trauma and how a child may internalize that pain, how they may birth terrifying monsters in their mind to help explain the horrors of the world around them.

"The House of Laments"
This story was inspired in part by the two years I lived in South Dakota. It was a shock to me, being a California native. There is a lot of farmland, dilapidated farmsteads, snow, and endless prairie. Under the wide-open skies at night, these things can seem frightening. Your mind wanders about the things lurking in that darkness. In those houses lying in shambles on the plains.

"Caravan"
This is a story about survival. If we begin with the premise that there is no morality—no right or wrong in the universe—then, our basest instinct as humans is to survive at any cost. Time and again we read about migrant caravans that embark on dangerous treks through Mexico, just to reach the United States. Groups of asylum seekers, political refugees, people looking for a better life for their families. People that include Central Americans, South Americans, Mexicans, and Caribbean refugees, among others. And every day these migrants get sick, die, get deported, or become accosted by opportunistic narcos and human traffickers. This story is also about a mother's love for her child, which I find to be one of the most powerful bonds.

"Body of Work; or, The Fever Dreams of a Parasite"
My Ligottian fashion horror story. The story is told in the form of a magazine article spotlighting a reclusive fashion designer looking to leave a lasting legacy before he dies. I was inspired to write this after binge-watching a few seasons of Project Runway. There are some tremendously talented designers creating some fantastic works of art, even if none of it appeals to me personally. Much respect to people who design and create clothing for a living. They put their blood, sweat, and tears into all they do.

"Effigies of Monstrous Things"
Minorities tend to get taken advantage of in the United States. They suffer infractions that seldom get reported. Tiny, invisible crimes that can ruin a person's life. That bank loan that was denied, the job offer that got turned down, the leaky pipe in your

subsidized housing unit that'll never get fixed. These are some of the issues I wanted to tackle in this story, under the framing of cosmic horror.

"The Body Booth"
I've always been a fan of David Cronenberg and this novelette is my homage to the great director. A tale of motherhood and body horror wherein a doctor of regenerative medicine creates a phone booth and living tissue hybrid for the purpose of birthing art. And maybe a little more.

"Postcards from Saguaroland"
This is another story about an ex-sicario. I love stories about broken people seeking redemption. They retain small flickers of light in the darkness of their hearts. Here, the story is told backwards, beginning at the end with the visceral corporeal terrors that we have come to expect from a horror story. It leads us to the ending, which is where the story begins chronologically, and reveals there is a terror far worse than any creature not born of this world.

Note: Some or all of the text from the notes for "Nightmare of a Million Faces," "Skins," and "Purveyors and Puppets," originally appeared in Nightmare Magazine #s 132 and 114, and A Night of Screams: Latino Horror Stories, respectively.

Previously Published

"Nightmare of a Million Faces," originally published in Nightmare Magazine #132, 2023.

"Feast of the Dreamer," originally published in Never Wake: An Anthology of Dream Horror, edited by Kenneth W. Cain & Time Meyer, Crystal Lake Publishing, 2023.

"Skins," originally published in Nightmare Magazine #114, 2022.

"Shantytown: A Mexican Ghost Story," originally published in Dread Imaginings, 2022.

"Purveyors and Puppets," originally published in A Night of Screams: Latino Horror Stories, edited by Richard Z. Santos, Arte Publico Press, 2023.

"Roots in Kon Tum," originally published in Stories We Tell After Midnight Vol. 3, edited by Rachel A. Brune, Crone Girls Press, 2021.

"Midnight Frequencies," originally published in Shortwave Magazine, 2022.

"The Cellar," is original to this collection.

"The Savage Night," originally published in The Lost Librarian's Grave, edited by Ann Wycoff, Redwood Press, 2021.

"The Bottom-Dweller," originally published in Tales from OmniPark, edited by Ben Thomas, House Blackwood, 2021.

"Adrift Ebon Tides," originally published in Anterior Skies Vol. 1, edited by C.F. Page, Strange Elf Press, 2023.

"Midnight Shoeshine," originally published in Twenty Twenty, edited by Ben Thomas & D Kershaw, Black Hare Press, 2020.

"The Last Train out of Calico," originally published in Along Harrowed Trails, edited by Beverly Bernard, Ashely Cranatas, & C.R. Langille, Timber Ghost Press, 2023.

"Bad Dogs," originally published in Bloodless, edited by Ben Walker, Sliced Up Press, 2022.

"Birthday Boy," originally published in Cape Cod Poetry Review, 2023.

"The House of Laments," originally published in Tales from the Clergy: Stories Inspired by Ghost, edited by Mark Scioneaux, October Nights Press, 2023.

"Caravan," originally published in Tiny Nightmares, edited by Lincoln Michel & Nadxieli Nieto, Catapult, 2020.

"Body of Work; or, The Fever Dreams of a Parasite," is original to this collection.

"Effigies of Monstrous Things," originally published in Beyond the Bounds of Infinity, edited by Vaughn A. Jackson & Stephanie Pearre, Raw Dog Screaming Press, 2024.

"The Body Booth," is original to this collection.

"Postcards from Saguaroland," originally published in Shadows Over Main Street Volume Three, edited by Doug Murano & D Alexander Ward, Bleeding Edge Books, 2023.

Acknowledgments

Thanks to:

Jennifer Barnes, for believing in these stories; Stephanie Pearre, for polishing my words and making the editing process a painless experience; Cynthia Pelayo for her wonderful introduction; Nuzo Onoh, Ai Jiang, Laird Barron, Theodore C. Van Alst Jr, and Nicholas Belardes, for their kind blurbs; Chloe, for supporting me through it all; My mother, Maria, my father, Pedro, and my sister, Sylvia, for their love; Dennis Etchison for putting me on this path; Every editor who has helped make me a stronger writer; Fellow authors who have inspired me to elevate my craft and reach for the stars; Every publisher that has taken a chance on me or offered an opportunity; Every supporter who has cheered me on and read my work. I love you all. Now and always.

About the Author

Pedro Iniguez is a horror and science-fiction writer from Los Angeles, California. He is a Rhysling Award finalist and a Pushcart Prize nominee.

He is the author of *Mexicans on the Moon: Speculative Poetry from a Possible Future*. His work has also appeared in *Nightmare Magazine*, *Never Wake: An Anthology of Dream Horror*, *Shadows Over Main Street Volume 3*, *Qualia Nous Vol. 2*, and *Beyond the Bounds of Infinity*, among others.

Forthcoming, his horror comic, *Catrina's Caravan: Blood Cycles* (Chispa Comics), and his SFF collection, *Echoes and Embers: Speculative Stories* (Stars and Sabers Publishing), are slated for 2025 releases.

www.ingramcontent.com/pod-product-compliance
Lightning Source LLC
Chambersburg PA
CBHW031236260626
47169CB00007B/2316